I put out a distress call with no expectation of recovering control.

Ravashan grunted and began hitting switches. Hanig turned up the cabin coolers and began clearing his side of the instrument board. I picked up the communicater and yelled to Selmon to hurry up and get the after bulkhead hatch. He was searing his hands on the hatch coaming.

Selmon threw himself into his chair, blowing blindly on his hands. I reached over and fastened his crash-straps for him, and cranked our two chairs into the three-quarter angle prescribed in the hardlanding procedures manual. The chaplain was moaning down at his lap. He looked like a monster, writhing against his straps.

Ravashan was setting us down. We skipped once, snapping and drumming inside, bottomed on the mud with brown water and bits of vegetation and smashed turtle foaming back over the viewport, swirling around in concentric spirals . . .

★   ★   ★

"THE BEST SCIENCE FICTION AUTHOR SINCE H. G. WELLS."
—**Kingsley Amis**

ALGIS BUDRYS
HARD LANDING

WARNER BOOKS

A Time Warner Company

WARNER BOOKS EDITION

Copyright © 1993 by Algis Budrys
All rights reserved.

Questar is a registered trademark of Warner Books, Inc.

Hand lettering by David Gatti
Cover illustration by David Mattingly
Cover design by Don Puckey

Warner Books, Inc.
1271 Avenue of the Americas
New York, NY 10020

W A Time Warner Company

Printed in the United States of America

First Printing: March, 1993

10 9 8 7 6 5 4 3 2 1

DEDICATION:
Judy Lynn del Rey, an editor

ACKNOWLEDGMENT:
Brian Thomsen, a very patient editor

CARD OF THANKS:
Betty Smith and Eric Wegner, two invaluable hands

DISCLAIMER:
Everything that follows is a lie.
Especially, of course, the parts that seem real.

PART OF A REPORT LATER REMOVED FROM THE AO/LGM FILE ON NEVILLE SEALMAN

The electrocuted man was found dead on the northbound tracks of the Borrow Street station of the Chicago Transit Authority suburban line in Shoreview, Illinois.

Shoreview is a city of 80,000 located on the Lake Michigan western shore immediately north of Chicago. For our purposes here, it can be regarded simply as a place where middle-class Chicago employees sleep and do their weekend errands.

It was early March and the time was 5:50 P.M. . . . a dark, chilled, wet evening. No witnesses to the death of the individual calling himself Neville Sealman have come forward.

Despite the occurrence on CTA property, the Shoreview Police Department took jurisdiction and investigated. (The CTA police force is strictly a peacekeeping body). Sergeant Dothan Stablits of the Shoreview PD was assigned. Before the body was moved, a representative of the CTA legal department arrived, and was extended cooperation by investigator Stablits. They went through the decedent's pockets together.

The contents supported identification of the decedent as Neville Unruh Sealman, a resident of south Shoreview. Documentation included an Illinois state driver's license and Social Security and Blue Cross cards found in his unrifled wallet, which also contained a normal amount of cash.

Social Security files later revealed the number had been issued against a falsified application. The driver's license had been properly acquired so far as procedures at the Illinois examining station went. (The decedent, however, never owned a car.) Records show the applicant identified himself at the time with a certified copy of Neville Sealman's birth certificate, which seems to have been acquired through the now well-known method of searching small-town newspaper obituaries for the names of persons dead in infancy. [Neville Unruh Sealman, b.–d. 1932, Mattoon, Ill.] The decedent's thirtyish appearance was consistent with the claimed age of 43 on the license.

The body was turned over to the Cook County coroner's office and a search for next of kin was instituted. (None were ever located; no friends were found, and no one who had been acquainted with the decedent any longer than the forty-two months of his residence and employment in the Chicago area. All the decedent's acquaintances were fellow employees or neighbors.)

Investigation at Sealman's home address—an apartment four stops before the stop where the body was found—developed the information that Sealman lived alone and unvisited in a furnished one-and-one-half-room efficiency. Any clues found in the apartment all supported the Sealman identity, and none of them were older than the time of Sealman's successful application for employment at Magnussen Engineering Co.

Magnussen is a free-lance drafting shop in a Chicago loft, and the requirement for filling a job opening is the ability to demonstrate standard proficiency at the craft; a Social Security number is the only document required of a prospective employee. No further information of any kind relating to his identity was ever found. His dwelling was unusually bare of knickknacks and personality. Nothing was found to indicate that he had ever been treated by any medical or dental facility, and this proved to be a matter of some concern in the initial investigation. (See further.)

Inquiry by Dothan Stablits at Magnussen indicated Sealman had been employed there since purportedly moving from Oakland, Cal. On the day of his death, he had left work at 5:00 P.M. as usual and boarded the Shoreview Express at the elevated State Street platform of the CTA. The northbound platform is visible from the windows of his place of employment, and he was observed in this action by his employer, who also described him as a steady, hardworking individual with nervous mannerisms and a lack of sociability.

Sealman's apartment was in due course released to the building management, and the personal contents transferred to the Cook County coroner's warehouse, where they remain unclaimed. Sergeant Stablits's report accurately describes them as items of clothing and personal care products purchasable at chain outlets in the Chicago/Shoreview vicinity. [A copy of that report is attached.] [Attachment 6]

Sergeant Stablits's Occurrence Report [Attachment 1] reflects a certain degree of uneasiness with the circumstances of the decedent's death.

The Borrow Street station is located in a purely residential section. The timing indicates Sealman must have ridden directly past his normal stop, but Stablits was unable to ascribe a reason for his doing so. Despite publicity in the Chicago news media and in the weekly *Shoreview Talk* newspaper, no one ever reported Sealman missing from an intended visit. Sergeant Stablits (now Chief Stablits of the Gouldville, Indiana, Police Department) clearly felt that this loose end impeded a satisfactory clearance of Sealman's file. But despite Sealman's insufficient bona fides, there was nothing actually inconsistent with a finding of accidental death, and no compelling reason to expend further resources and press the investigation further—for instance, out of state to Oakland. When the FBI proved to have no record of his fingerprints, his file, though not closed, was simply kept available in the event some fresh occurrence might reactivate it. No such event took place.

The CTA legal department at first took a more than routine interest in the case. The Borrow Street station dates from 1912. It is located in a deep open cut well below the level of adjacent streets and dwellings, the right-of-way north of the Chicago elevated structures having gradually gone to street level and then below. This secluded location added to the unlikelihood of finding a witness to explain Sealman's death. It's safe to say the CTA was anticipating a negligence lawsuit by heirs.

Portions of the station structure have weathered to a rickety condition, and it is scheduled to be completely rebuilt in 1981. The condition of the platform is decrepit. Half the platform lights are not functional, and the exit stairs up to street level, cast in reinforced concrete and subject to extreme weathering action once the surface had spalled away to the included rust-prone steel, are frankly hazardous.

(The CTA operates at a loss, and is seeking some sort of public subsidy. Its trackage and equipment include property acquired from inefficient predecessor operating authorities and bankrupt private traction companies.)

Despite the nonappearance of immediate potential litigants, the CTA felt that all possible steps should be taken to exclude the possibility of the decedent's having tripped, fallen to the tracks, and contacted the third rail as the result of some structural feature of the platform. Frankly, that seemed an obvious possibility, but a history of cardiovascular disorders in Sealman, or some other cause of chronic vertigo, would have done much to brighten up the CTA's files. Almost as satisfactory would have been evidence to support a finding of probable suicide, or even of foul play. On none of these possibilities was Sergeant Stablits able to turn up anything that would help.

On finding there were no medical or dental offices located within reasonable distance of the stop, he made no further effort to locate any medical practitioner who might have had Sealman as a patient. His interest was limited to finding a reason for Sealman's presence on that platform that night, and he indicated to the CTA that if they wanted to check with every doctor in the Chicago area, they could do that on their own budget. After this time, the CTA and Shoreview PD efforts continued separately (and terminated inconclusively separately).

In this atmosphere, a number of private as well as official communications were exchanged between the CTA, the Cook County medical examiner's office, and individuals therein acting on an informal basis. As a consequence, the medical examiner's office assigned its most experienced forensics pathologist to the autopsy, and that individual proceeded with great care and attention to detail.

Soon after beginning his examination of the thoracic cavity, this pathologist—Albert Camus, M.D.—notified the medical examiner that he was encountering noteworthy anomalies. The procedure was then confidentially completed in the presence of the medical examiner, and certain administrative decisions were then made.

The findings filed were consistent with death by electrocution and no other cause, which was in fact true according to the evidence, and the CTA was so notified. At some point, it must have become increasingly clear that no legatees were in the offing, so the CTA may not have taken Dr. Camus's official report as hard as it would have a few days sooner. In any event, the CTA's file has subsequently been marked inactive, and there has been no change in that status.

The medical examiner's file, however, reflects the great number of confusions raised by the pathologist's discovery of what he described as "a high-capacity, high-pressure" cardiovascular system, as well as a number of other significant and anatomically consistent variations from the norm. [Attachment 2]

At Dr. Camus's suggestion, a telephone call was placed to this office,* with the objective of determining whether these findings were unique.

On receipt of the call here, a case officer (under-signed) was immediately allocated by the Triage Section, and put on the line. A request was made to the Cook County medical examiner for a second autopsy, and Dr. William Henshaw, a resource of this office, was dispatched to Shoreview via commercial air transportation. [Attachment 7, Voucher of Expenses]

At the same time, an AO/LGM Notification was forwarded to our parent organization. (EXCERPT ENDS)

NOTE: CASE OFFICER'S SIGNATURE
ILLEGIBLE

---

*The National Register of Pathological Anomalies, Washington, D.C.

AUTHOR'S NOTE ON THE NATIONAL REGISTER OF PATHOLOGICAL ANOMALIES

The National Register of Pathological Anomalies is federally funded and was formed in the late 1940s. It publishes bulletins to tax-supported pathological services and other interested parties. This information is restricted to describing unusual anatomical structures and functions found in the course of routine postmortem examinations.

There are a number of "usual" anomalies, and the NRPA doesn't concern itself with them. Quite a few people have their hearts located toward the right side of the chest, or are born without a vermiform appendix. Extra fingers and toes, and anomalous genitalia, are other everyday examples. One of the earliest things a medical student learns is that the details of any given human being's internal arrangements will be roughly similar to but teasingly different from the tidy diagrams in the textbooks. This happens without impairing the individual's general function as a clearly, understandably human and essentially healthy organism. Anatomy classes dispel any notion that God works with a cookie cutter. The idea they do create is that the mechanisms of life are both subtler and more determined to proceed than most people can imagine. In many cases, these anomalies are successful enough so that they're never noted during the individual's lifetime. Since most deaths are not followed by autopsies, there are no reliable statistics on how prevalent all this might be.

What this does mean is that there are any number of individuals walking around who will respond peculiarly to conventional medical and surgical treatment, who might overcome what ought to be disabling or fatal injuries while succumbing to apparently minor accidents, or who might even be able to evade normal methods of restraint and punishment—to name a few areas of intense interest to authorities charged with the maintenance of the public health and good order.

The NRPA publications concern themselves only with extreme cases. They also draw exact distinctions between kinds of extreme. There are what might be called man-made anomalies; defects almost certainly created by actions of various manufactured substances upon the individual's mother during her pregnancy. These, while not completely cataloged, are part of a distinct field of medical investigation that's keeping reasonable pace with the ingenuities of recreational drug use and the pyramiding effects of modern industrial chemistry. The NRPA describes apparent cases in this category when they're found, and this reason alone suffices to make its bulletins widely studied. But there is another category.

Occasionally, an autopsy will turn up organs, or even systems of organs, that are truly unique and whose function, in fact, may not be understandable to the resources of the pathologist who discovers them. The NRPA is very quick to react positively in such cases. At once, it will give the examiner all the help and information humanly possible, and join in delving into the matter thoroughly. As a result of its reputation for this sort of help, always welcomed even by pathology departments that have been nominally well funded, the NRPA's twenty-four-hour phone number is kept very much in mind throughout all nations signatory to the cross-cooperation agreements fostered by the World Health Organization.

It should be understood that almost invariably, one mundane explanation or the other is finally found for the seeming anomaly displayed by the particular case.

The NRPA's annual budget is drawn against funds made available by Congress to a parent organization. This form of second-derivative funding is common in cases where the parent organization is the Central Intelligence Agency, the Federal Bureau of Investigation, or the National Security Agency, to name just three. It hasn't been possible for me to determine the NRPA's parent organization.

AO stands for "anomalous organs." Most NRPA files are headed with the AO prefix followed by a number coded to show the date the file was opened and predict when it might be closed. These files form the basis for most of the material in the bulletins, and are of unquestionable immediate value to medical specialists dealing with the results of human interactions.

A far lesser portion of the files is headed AO/LGM, in which the second set of initials in the prefix is said to represent "less germane matters." Access to and use of these files is restricted to the top echelons of NRPA. An AO/LGM Notification—at one time a slip printed on red paper, now an advice preceded by a special tone signal on the NRPA's computerized communications devices, which connect to God knows where—is required the instant a new file in this category is opened. At NRPA, which is housed in a three-story red brick Georgian with a very nice little company café under the trees in the backyard, there's an office joke that LGM really stands for Little Green Men.

—A.B.

PRELUDE TO EVENTS EARLY ON A MARCH EVENING

Jack Mullica had almost stopped being annoyed with Selmon for riding the same train with him. It had now been three and a half years since he had first seen Selmon standing at the other end of the State Street northbound platform in the five-o'clock sunshine of late September.

It had been nothing like it was in the winter when the wind they called the Hawk hunted through the Loop. The people among whom the two men stood had their heads up, and did not jockey to take shelter behind each other on the elevated platform.

Their eyes met across an interval of some ten yards, and Selmon's mouth dropped open. Not until he saw the stranger's reaction did Mullica fully realize what had been naggingly familiar about him. Mullica watched a look of total defeat come over Selmon. He stood there, shorter and a little chubbier than Mullica remembered him, his head now down, his herringbone topcoat suddenly too big for him, a briefcase hanging from one hand, a *Daily News* from the other. He didn't even board the train. He stayed where he was, washed by low-angle sunlight and forlorn, thunderstruck, waiting at least for the next train, not looking in the window as Mullica rode by him.

But the next night he had boarded, and hadn't gotten off until just a few stops before Mullica's, staring rigidly ahead and keeping his shoulders stiff. It had become a regular thing. Selmon rode as many cars away from Mullica as he could. He was there almost every night Mullica was. Mullica traveled out of town fairly frequently. He assumed Selmon didn't, though at first he watched carefully behind him in airline terminals and out at motels. But Selmon never turned up anywhere else and he never made any attempt at an approach. After a while Mullica decided that was how it was going to be.

Gradually, thinking about it in the slow, schooled way he had taught himself, Mullica reached an accommodation with the situation. He assumed that Selmon had simply happened to take a job nearby, and that the rest of it was natural enough; it was all coincidence, Selmon's working near Mullica and living in the same town with Mullica and his wife, Margery.

The Shoreview Express was designed to handle North Shore traffic in and out of the Loop. Once it had made all the Loop stops, picking up shoppers on the east and south sides, and management types on the west and north, it paused at the Merchandise Mart and then didn't stop again until Loyola University. It rumbled directly over the worst parts of the North Side on girdered elevated tracks, and then imperceptibly began running on a solid earthen viaduct through blue-collar and then lower-middle-class residential neighborhoods. The farther north it ran, the more respectable its environment became and the more out of place the shabby old string of riveted iron cars appeared, until it reached the end of Chicago at Howard Street, entered Shoreview as an all-stops local, and began to look quaint.

Its first Shoreview stop was Elm Shore Avenue, in an area only slightly distinguishable from the red-brick northernmost part of Chicago, and this was where Selmon got off. Mullica lived in a white and yellow high rise near the Borrow Street stop, which the train reached rattling over switch points, its collector shoes arcing, flashing, and sputtering over gaps in the third rail system; at night it rode through sheets of violet fire. The train's next and last destination was in Wilmette, which was yet another municipality and where one could begin to see the prewar money living in its rows of increasingly large and acreage-enshrouded mansions all the way up the lakefront for miles. From Wilmette and beyond, they usually drove into the city in cars suitable for after-nine arrivals, or took the North Western Rail Road and smoked and played bridge.

Mullica's hours in the Chicago public relations office of one of the major automobile manufacturers were nominally nine to five. He usually got in about nine-fifteen, getting back some of the three A.M.s on the road. He never saw Selmon in the morning; probably he had to be at work by eight-thirty.

At night on the platform, Selmon would open his paper as soon as he was through the turnstile. He would read it at his end of the platform, holding it in front of his face. Mullica would stand just where he had stood every time since years before Selmon. Mullica opened his paper on the train, and when he was nearly finished, the sound of the wheels echoing back would tell him they were off the viaducts and beginning to run between the weed-grown cutbanks of the right-of-way in north Shoreview. He'd fold his paper, get up from the warped, timeworn cane seat, and go stand in the chipped brown vestibule waiting for the uncertain brakes to drag the train to a halt. He'd get off, walk the three blocks to the condominium, greet Margery if she was home, have a drink looking out over the lake with a closed expression, and do the crossword puzzle in ink before throwing the paper out. He wished Selmon would play by the rules and move away. But Selmon wouldn't. He continued to work somewhere in the Loop at something, and to live somewhere two miles south.

AN OCCURRENCE EARLY ON A MARCH EVENING

Mullica never saw Selmon in Shoreview on weekends. Margery liked to go shopping in the big malls at Old Orchard and Golf Mill; Mullica had a Millionaires' Club membership, and sometimes they'd sit there after shopping, sipping. Sometimes then Mullica would be able to just stare over Margery's shoulder and think about any number of things. At times, he thought of Selmon. He wondered if he hid in his home on weekends, and if he had found a wife, and, if so, how they got along. He wondered if Margery might run into her someday and if, by some coincidence, they might get friendly enough to talk about their husbands. But it seemed unlikely; Margery didn't get along with women.

And then it was early March, forty-two months since Selmon had turned up. Mullica stood on the platform, his hands deep in his pockets. It was a cold, raw day. He watched Selmon stubbornly unfolding his paper against the wind, and clutching it open as he began to read. Then, just as their train began to pull into the station, Selmon saw something in the paper that made him turn his face toward Mullica in the twilight in a white blur of dismay, his mouth a dark open oval, and Mullica thought for a minute Selmon had felt a vessel exploding in his brain.

The train pulled up and Mullica stepped aboard. He moved down the aisle and took a seat next to a window. He looked out at Selmon's spot as the train passed by it, thinking he might see Selmon lying there huddled in a crowd, but he wasn't there.

Mullica put his zipcase across his knees and opened his paper, sitting there reading from front to back as he always did, while the train crossed the river toward the Merchandise Mart. He stopped to look eastward along the river, as he always did, year round, enjoying the changing light of the seasons on the buildings and the water and horizon. The riverfront buildings were just turning into boxes of nested light, their upper story glass still reflecting the last streaks of dying pink from the sunset, and the stars were beginning to appear in the purplish black sky above the lake.

Page two had the story:

Not-So-Ancient Astronauts?
"THING" IN JERSEY SWAMP IS SAUCER,
EXPERT SAYS

PHILADELPHIA, MARCH 9 (AP)—Swamp-draining crews in New Jersey may have found a spaceship, declared scientist Allen Wolverton today.

Authorities on the spot immediately denied that old bog land being readied for a housing development held anything mysterious.

Local authorities agreed a domed, metal object, fifty feet across, was dragged from the soil being reclaimed from Atlantic coastal marshes. They quickly pointed out, however, that there is a long history of people living in the swamps, described as the last rural area remaining on the Eastern Seaboard between Boston and Virginia.

The area was populated and prosperous in Colonial times, the center of a thriving "bog iron" mining industry. Local experts were quick to point to this as the likely source of the object, citing it as some sort of machinery or a storage bin.

"There was whole towns and stagecoach stops back in there once," said Henry Stemmler, operator of a nearby crossroads grocery store. "Big wagon freight yards and everything. There's all kinds of old stuff down in the bogs."

Dissenting is Wolverton, a lecturer at Philadelphia's Franklin Planetarium. "Our earth is only one of thousands of inhabitable planets," he declared. "Statistically, the galaxy must hold other

intelligent races. It would be unreasonable to suppose at least one of them isn't visiting us and
surreptitiously observing our progress toward either an enlighted civilization of peace and love or
total self-destruction.''

There was a blurred two-column wire photo of two
men standing in some underbrush, staring at a curved
shape protruding from the ground. There were no
clearly defined features, and the object's outline was
broken by blending into the angular forms of a dredge
in the background. It might have been anything—the
lid of a large silo, part of an underground oil tank, or
the work of a retoucher's brush. In fact, the paper's
picture editor had obviously decided the wire photo
would reproduce badly and had his artist do some outlin-
ing and filling. So the result was a considerable percent-
age away from reality.

Mullica read the other stories on the page, and on the
next page, and turned it.

It was night when the train reached Borrow Street—
full dark, with only a few working bulbs in chipped old
white enamel lamps to light the winter-soaked, rotting
old wooden platform.

It's all going to hell, Mullica thought. No one main-
tains anything that isn't absolutely vital, but the fare
keeps going up and up.

No one manned the station except during morning
rush hour on the southbound side. The cement steps

from the northbound platform up to the frontage street were a forty-foot gravel slide with broken reinforcing bars protruding through it rustily to offer the best foot-holds.

Mullica began to move toward the exit gates in the middle of the platform, lining up with the others who'd gotten off. They were all head-down, huddling against the wind, concentrating their minds on getting through the revolving metal combs of the gate and picking their way up the incline. And then because he had not quite put it all out of his mind, and his skin was tight under the hairs of his body, he had the feeling to turn his head. When he did, he saw Selmon still standing where he had gotten off, his paper half-raised toward Mullica, his apparition coming and going in the passing window lights as the train went on. Mullica could see he was about to call out a name nobody knew.

Mullica stopped, and the small crowd flowed around him inattentively. He walked back to Selmon. "They'll find us!" Selmon blurted. "They'll trace us down!"

Mullica looked at him carefully. Then he said "How will they do that?" picking and arranging the words with care, the language blocky on his tongue. He watched Selmon breathe spasmodically, his mouth quivering. He saw that Selmon was years younger than he—though they were the same age—and soft. And yet there was advanced deterioration in him. It was in the shoulders and the set of the head, and very much in the eyes, as well. Selmon clutched at his arm as they stood alone on the platform. Selmon's hand moved more rapidly than one would expect, but slowly for one of their kind of people, and uncertainly.

"Arvan, it's bound to happen," Selmon insisted to him. "They—they have evidence." He pushed the paper forward. Mullica ignored it.

"No, Selmon," he said as calmly as he could. "They won't know what to do with it. There's nothing they can learn from it. The engines melted themselves, and we destroyed the instruments before we left it, remember?"

"But they have the hull, Arvan! Real metal you can touch; hit with a hammer. A real piece of evidence. How can they ignore that?"

"Come on. Their investigators constantly lie to their own populace and file their secrets away. They systematically ridicule anyone who wants to look for us, and they defame them." Mullica was trying to think of how to deal with this all. He wanted Selmon to cross over to the deserted southbound platform and go home to his wife. Mullica wanted to go home; even to have a drink with Margery, and then sit in his den reading the specification sheets on the new product. It was some twenty-five years since he'd been a navigator.

"Arvan, what are we going to do? How can you ignore this?" Selmon wouldn't let go of Mullica's forearm, and his grip was epileptically tight. He peered up into Mullica's face. "You're old, Arvan," he accused. "You look like one of them. That haircut. Those clothes. All mod. A middle-aged macho. You're becoming like them!"

"I live among . . . them."

"I should have spoken to you years ago!"

"You shouldn't be speaking to me at all. Why are you here? There's the entire United States. There's the whole world, if you can find your way across a border. A whole world, just a handful of us, and you stay here!"

Selmon shook his head. "I was in Oakland for a long time. Then I bumped into Hanig on a street in San Francisco. He told me to go away, too."

"He spoke to you?" Mullica asked sharply.

"He had to. He—he wanted me out of there. He'd been in the area less time than I had, but he had a business, and a family, and I was alone."

"A family."

"He married a widow with children and a store—a fish store. So I agreed to leave. He gave me some money, and I came to Chicago."

Well, if navigators could write public relations copy, copilots could sell fish. What did engineering officers do to make their way in this world? Mullica wondered, but Selmon gave him no opportunity to ask.

"Hanig had seen Captain Ravashan. In passing. He didn't think Ravashan saw him. In Denver. That was why he left there and came to San Francisco. And then I came to Chicago, and almost the first week, I saw you. I—I think we're too much alike when we react to this world. We wander toward the same places, and move in the same ways."

"Does anyone know where the chaplain is?" Mullica asked quickly.

"Chaplain Joro?" Selmon asked. He and Mullica looked into each other's eyes. "No, I don't think there's much doubt," and for a moment there was a bond of complete understanding between the two of them. Mullica nodded. For over a quarter of a century, he saw, Selmon as well as he had reflected on the matter. It had seemed to him for a long time that there were only four of them now.

Selmon looked up at him in weariness. "It's no use, Arvan. I—" he hung his head, "I have a good job. It doesn't pay much but I don't need much, and it's secure. So I decided to stay. You never asked me to leave." There were tears in his eyes. "I'm very tired, Arvan," he whispered, and Mullica saw the guilt in him, waiting to be punished.

But there was no telling whether any engineering officer could have solved the problem with the engines. Mullica had never thought much of Selmon, but Ditlo Ravashan never questioned his ability in front of the rest of them, and there hadn't been any backbiting after the crash.

"This isn't anything, Selmon. There'll be a flurry, but it'll blow over. Somebody'll write another one of those books—that planetarium lecturer, probably—and everyone with any common sense will laugh at it."

"But they've never had evidence before!" He was almost beating at Mullica with his newspaper, waving his free arm. "Now they do!"

"How do you know what they have or haven't had? They must have. They have enough films, and enough unexplained things in their history. They must have other pieces of crashed or jettisoned equipment, too. They just don't know how to deal with them. And they won't know how to deal with this, either.''

''Arvan! An intact hull, and instruments obviously destroyed after the landing! A ship buried in a swamp. Buried, Arvan—not driven into the ground. And five empty crew seats behind an open hatch!''

''A hull full of mud. If they ever shovel it all out, it'll be weeks . . . and all those weeks, their bureaucracy will be working on everyone to forget it.''

''Arvan, I don't understand you! Don't you care?''

''Care? I was a navigator in the stars.''

''And what are you now?''

''What are you, Selmon?'' Mullica pushed him away, but Selmon still clung to his arm. They staggered on the platform.

''Arvan, we have to plan. We have to find the others and plan together,'' he begged, weeping.

''Four of us together,'' Mullica said, saying the number aloud for the first time, hearing his voice harsh and disgusted, aching deeper in his throat than he had become accustomed to speaking. ''So they can have us all—a complete operating crew. An engineer, a navigator who knows the courses, a pilot, and a copilot lifesystems man. To go with the hull and their industrial capacity. You want us to get together, so they can find us and break out uncontrolled in our domains.''

Four men with similarly odd configurations of their wrists and ankles. Four men with similar skin texture.

Four men with high blood pressure and a normal body temperature of 100; with hundreds of idiosyncrasies in cell structure, blood typing, and, most certainly, chromosome structure. Four such men in a room, secretively discussing something vital in a language no one spoke.

"Arvan!"

"Goddamn it, Selmon, let go of me!" Mullica shouted in English. "Fuck off!"

Selmon jerked backward. He stared as if Mullica had slashed his throat, and as he stepped backward he pushed Mullica away, pushing himself back. His mouth was open again.

Hopeless, hopeless, Mullica thought, trying to regain his balance so he could reach for Selmon, watching Selmon's wounded eyes, his newspaper fanning open ridiculously, stepping back with one heel on thin air.

He hit the tracks with a gasping outcry. Mullica jumped forward and looked down. Selmon sat sprawled over the rails, his paper scattered over the ties, in the greasy mud and the creosote-stained ballast, looking up at Mullica with the wind knocked out of him. The distant lights and violet sputtering of the next train were coming up the track from the previous station. Mullica squatted down to reach for him, holding out his hand. Selmon fumbled to push himself up, staring at Mullica. Neither spoke. Groping for something firm to grasp, Selmon put his hand on the third rail.

The flash and the gunlike crack threw Mullica down flat on the platform, nearly blind. But I think I will still be able to see him anytime, Mullica thought in his native language as he threw himself up to his feet and ran, ran faster than anyone had ever seen Jack Mullica run, caroming through the exit gate and up the weathered steps, realizing he had never at any time let go of his zipcase, and thinking, Now we are three.

TRANSCRIBED CONVERSATION; ALBERT CAMUS; WILLIAM HENSHAW:

CAMUS: You've seen one of these before, haven't you?

HENSHAW: Prob'ly. You know, I can never get used to how cold it gets in these places.

CAMUS: Rather have it cold than hot. Look, if you're going to let me assist you in the first place, talk to me, will you?

HENSHAW: I can talk some. And you can watch anythin' you can see. Can't at all limit you from thinking.

CAMUS: I can see you know exactly what to look for.

HENSHAW: What you see is somebody who knows what to expect. What to look for may be somethin' else again.

CAMUS: Well-made point, Doctor.

HENSHAW: Reach me that thing over there, will you?

CAMUS: You know, if I saw him on the street, I wouldn't think twice. But now look at that.

HENSHAW: You'd figure that jaw came from a malocclusion, right? And that skin color—just like a normal Caucasian maybe a little toward the extreme with his oxygen metabolism, right? But now you take some of them scrapin's and stick 'em under a microscope, and—

CAMUS: Yes, I've done that.

HENSHAW: Figured. That's why I let you stay. Might as well. Here—you see that wrist? What do you figure that to be?

CAMUS: A thick wrist. I never would look at it.

HENSHAW: Yeah. But let's just flap this back a little, and—

CAMUS: Holy cats!

HENSHAW: Right. There's your proximal row. You see that bone? That's what he's got instead of a navicular. Great blood supply, too. First of all, he can't break it anywhere near as readily as people do. Second, if it breaks, it heals nice and slick. But how does he break it? Look at all those cushions in the cartilaginous structure. And let me tell you something else—all the joints are engineered like that. These people don't get arthritis, they don't get sprains, they maybe once in a blue moon get breaks. It's like those teeth: never seen a dentist's drill. This is a healthy, healthy guy.

CAMUS: And it all still fits inside a normal shape, more or less.

HENSHAW: Fits exactly. He's the normal shape for what he is.

CAMUS: What is he?

HENSHAW: You know, down in South America lots of millions of years ago, they had things that were shaped almost exactly like camels, but they weren't mammals, they were marsupials, and their skeletons weren't put together like camel skeletons. I went to that museum they have down there in Guayaquil and looked at some of those bones; looked stranger than anything we've got lying here in front of us today. But once the musculature was on the bone, and the hide was on the muscles, if you saw that thing walk out from behind a rock at you, it was a camel. They had tigers like that, too. Things evolve to fit needs in the ecology. Life needed camels in the high-altitude deserts, and the camels needed tigers to prey on them. Time passed, they went away. Now down there they got llamas and guanacos and jaguars, and if some marsupial medico had to take 'em apart, wouldn't he be surprised.

CAMUS:	This guy is a mammal.
HENSHAW:	Well, yeah. You put him in a raincoat and boots, he can stand a short-arm check with everybody else in the platoon, no doubtin' that.
CAMUS:	What's next, doctor?
HENSHAW:	No sense goin' any further here. He checks out for type. And I've got my tissue and blood samples to take back to my lab, so I'd better get goin'. Somebody'll be around to pick him up in a couple of hours. They'll give you a receipt for him. I don't think you'll get any grieving relatives. If anybody does come around and ask for him, stall and call the hotline. You'll get quick relief.
CAMUS:	I have to have the coroner's okay before I can give him to you.
HENSHAW:	No problem. I brought a letter with me.
CAMUS:	Now what?
HENSHAW:	How do you mean?
CAMUS:	What do I have to sign? What sort of oath do I swear?
HENSHAW:	Hell, you're not going to mess up. You've got yourself a nice position here, lots of contacts with the local politics; family, property . . . all that good shit.
CAMUS:	I suppose so. You wouldn't happen to have an opening in your department?
HENSHAW:	My department?

CAMUS: Wherever you really come from.

HENSHAW: I really come from the NRPA, and I'm all
            the medical talent they need. This doesn't
            come up every day, you know. Besides,
            they wouldn't consider you qualified.
            Sorry.

CAMUS: I don't believe I've read any of your pa-
            pers, Doctor. Or run into you at pathology
            convention seminars. Where'd you get
            your training?

HENSHAW: Iowa. University of Iowa School of Veter-
            inary Medicine, Doctor.

LATER EVENTS ON A MARCH NIGHT

It was a nice condominum apartment: four and one-half rooms high enough up, with gold, avocado, and persimmon carpeting, French provincial furnishings from John M. Smythe, a patio balcony with sliding glass doors, swag lamps, and a Tandberg Dolby cassette system which he switched on automatically for warmth. Barbra Streisand sang "I'll Tell the Man in the Street."

Margery wasn't home. Mullica got some ice in a rocks glass, picked up the scotch decanter, and sat in the living room with the lights down. He sipped and looked out through the glass doors and past the wrought-iron balcony railing, at the lake. Below his line of sight were the tops of the as yet unbudded famous elms of Shoreview. Far down the lake shore curving out to his extreme right were the tall lighted embrasures of the Gold Coast high rises in Chicago.

He took a deep breath. What will happen? he thought.

Let's put it together. He began systematically reviewing the events on the Borrow Street platform. Then he pictured a detective in his trenchcoat kneeling beside the facedown body in the headlight from the stopped five-fifty train. He put dialogue in the detective's head to indicate what the detective might make of what there was to see. He listened critically. The ice cubes were cold against his upper lip.

The detective saw that Selmon had been electrocuted. He saw nothing to show that the dead man had been the victim of an assault. So it was clearly something that had happened by itself, an accident or suicide, and there was no need for an autopsy. Now the detective went through the dead man's pockets. If he'd done that to Jack Mullica, he wouldn't have found any connection to any abandoned bog iron works.

Selmon's identity wouldn't be particularly thin. He'd have a Social Security card so he could work, and probably a driver's license. He surely had a checking account, and it was practically impossible to convert checks into spot cash without a driver's license, even if you never drove.

Now the detective moved to Selmon's apartment. Again, there'd be nothing of any significance. Unless Selmon still had parts of his first-aid kit and was stupid enough to store them where he lived. But after more than twenty-five years, what would he have left, no matter how healthy he looked? No, it wouldn't be the presence of anything that bothered the detective. It would be absence. No military service records, no school diplomas.

Would that matter so much? It was just a routine investigation into a casual accident. What the hell? Still, they might get curious and push it some.

Barbra Streisand sang "Who's Afraid of the Big Bad Wolf?" Mullica refilled his glass.

If they were curious, how long would curiosity persist? Selmon hadn't been shot, or robbed, or hit behind the ear. All he was, really, was one of what had to be thousands of perfectly settled-down citizens who had chopped themselves free of something in their pasts that might make them unemployable. It seemed to Mullica that in a society where a high school marijuana bust or a college Red affiliation could haunt you to your grave, a lot of that had to be going on. Once you had figured a way of getting a set of papers in a new name—crime novels were full of ways that worked—you rarely had to stand up to a real bedrock investigation. Ordinarily they didn't check your identity; just your identity's credit.

The wife. Selmon's wife. Would he have talked to her? Would he have told this woman he was Engineering Officer Selmon, and that Navigator Arvan lived right up the tracks?

Well, did Margery have any inkling that Engineering Officer Selmon was riding the train with Navigator Arvan? And if she did, could she put a face to either name? No—Mullica shook his head—it was Jack Mullica that Margery knew dangerous things about.

Barbra Streisand sang "Soon It's Gonna Rain."

Mullica swallowed, and the cold, sweet scotch made his palate tingle. He refilled his glass.

Out beyond the elms and the floodlit, strut-supported balls of the Lindheimer Observatory on the Northwestern University lakefront campus were stars whose names he did not know in constellations he had never learned. From where Arvan sat now, he could see that the Shieldmaiden was as lanky as a *Vogue* model and the Howler's paws were awkwardly placed. All of those suns blazing in the night out there had names and catalog numbers in the local astronomy tables, but he had never learned them, except for the little bits that everyone knew. He knew the Big Dipper, and he knew how to find what they called Polaris. But let the locals come and wring him for how to find the places of his folk. If they ever became aware enough to do that, let them also learn to translate.

Jack Mullica felt that he looked out into the night sky only at controlled times.

Who said there was even a Mrs. Selmon? Would a married Selmon have moved so easily from Oakland just like that? Oh, hell, he'd even said he was alone in Oakland, hadn't he, and the Selmon trying to make himself invisible on Loop CTA platforms didn't seem the type to go courting around here.

Funny how the mind had registered that and yet not registered it. Face it, it was only because Mullica was married, of all unlikely things, that he had put his mind on that track. He couldn't imagine how one of them could get married except under the most extraordinary circumstances. It was funny the tricks your mind could play. . . . Oh, shit! Eikmo was married, too!—Eikmo and his fish-store lady—Mullica, what the hell good does your mind do you? But the important thing was they were probably in the clear—Navigator Arvan, and Hanig Eikmo, and Ditlo Ravashan, all three. Ravashan, he thought, would be in the clear in a cage full of tigers.

Barbra Streisand sang "Happy Days Are Here Again."

Still, he thought briefly of taking a personal ad in the Denver and San Francisco papers. "Olir Selmon RIP Chicagoland. All O.K. Dwuord Arvan." Something like that.

But when he thought about it some more, his lips and the tip of his nose pleasantly numb, it became clear that he was playing with his mind again. All he was trying to do was give the poor bastard an obituary notice, and none of them could have that.

He could point a high-frequency antenna upward and broadcast the news; all he had to do was go to Radio Shack and buy the hardware, with a promise to apply for the FCC license. And then if there happened to be somebody along the line of transmission, it might be one of his people who heard it, instead of a Methane-Breather or a local in the local "space program" monitoring a local satellite.

No, it was going to happen to each of them, in its own time, silently far from home and in a land of cool-blooded foreigners.

Poor clumsy bastard. Engineering trades graduate, exploration volunteer, parents living at last report, farm boy, originally—didn't like shoveling manure, one would guess, and turned his mind to ways of getting out of it. If you weren't in one of the academies, the only way to make officer status and then have some hope of getting up the promotion ladder was to go the route they'd all gone. And the bonus pay made a difference. But you didn't have much to talk about in letters home from the slick, modern metropolitan training center to the rural little outpost of your birth. Still, the parents were there at the graduation ceremony. Stolid folk with callused hands, their eyes wet and alive in the lights from the podium where you came up in your brand-new dress reds and held out your hand for the certificate. And now he was an accident among people who couldn't ship the body home.

Well, have another scotch alcohol, Jack Mullica, he said to himself, and turned up the light beside his chair.

Margery came home about eight o'clock. She was a good-looking, slim, long-legged frosted brunette just past forty but didn't look it, pointy-breasted, and she seemed a little flushed and swollen-lipped. She found Mullica sitting in the den with glossy photographs of a car model line spread on his desk beside the rocks glass.

"Hello. Did you eat?" she asked.

"I thawed something. You?"

"I'll make a hamburger, I guess. See the paper?"

"Read it on the train."

"They found something in the bog near where you first turned up."

"I saw that." He looked at her and let his smile widen crazily. "It's a piece of flying saucer, all right. For you see, darling, as I slip off this outer skin, you will know that you have come to love a being from another Solar System."

She snorted. "Oh, God." She came forward and tousled his hair. "I do love you, you know," she said fondly. "I really do." She raised an eyebrow, then looked at the pictures on his desk and the blank piece of paper in his typewriter. "Will you be up late?"

He nodded. "Detroit's having a rash of midyear models. Low-displacement engines, stick shifts, high rear-axle ratios. Arab-fighter product. Won't carry luggage, won't climb a hill, but we'll talk gas mileage. Detroit wants all the stops out with the local press; I've got to flange up some release copy, here, and start planning a junket out to a test track. Be in bed about midnight, I guess."

"All right. I'll watch TV for a while and go to sleep."

"Fine."

She stayed in the doorway for a moment. "When will the press conference be?"

"Soon. Has to be, if it's going to do any good for the summer. Do it up at Lake Geneva, probably— Playboy Hotel." He looked down at his hands. "Be gone four, five days. Finish up on a Friday." He waited.

She said: "I asked because Sally and I were talking

about going out to Arizona to that ranch she talks about. If you were going to be out of town anyway, that would be—"

"A good time for it. Right. I'll let you know as soon as we have firm dates."

She'd look good in tight jeans and a western shirt. Not as good as she'd have looked in her twenties, but there was a limit to how soon promotional copywriting could lead a man's wife into the habits of affluence. And it was immaterial how she might look in a Playboy Hotel room on a Friday night with a good week's work under your belt. "Good night. See you in the morning," he said.

"'Night." When she turned to go, he could see that her petticoat was twisted under her tailored black skirt, and the eyelet at the top of her zipper was unhooked at her neck. Her gleaming hair almost hid that.

He had met Margery's only woman friend, Sally. She was all right—a steady-eyed keypunch pool supervisor with a four-martini voice—and she was the type who always returned favors. Sally had a lot of contacts, a busy social schedule, and a life plan that wasn't anything Margery couldn't cover for her with a few alibi phone calls to Sally's various fiancés and good friends.

He went back to culling together specifications and making notes on a scratch pad. After a while, he turned to his typewriter and wrote, "Sporty but thrifty, the exciting new mid-year XF-1000 GT features the proven inline 240 C.I.D. six-cylinder Milemiser engine with . . ."

With what? With the simple fuel-saving carburetor and the uneven mixture distribution in the intake mani-fold, or with the space-age solid-state ignition that was the only thing that let the engine run at all with all those emission controls fucking over the power curve? He frowned and decided to list the electronics ahead of the single barrel; after a tongueful like Milemiser you wanted to come back fast with something sexy.

He went on with his work. He concentrated on being the best there was in Chicago. In his trade, the name of Jack Mullica meant something.

"Designed to take the Chicagoland family to even the most far-flung summer destination with a minimum of fuel cost, the XF-1000 GT's comfort features sacri-fice nothing. . . ."

THE RATIONALE*

We don't retrieve people. It's a good policy. You have to assume the down vehicle was being tracked. If another one now goes in after it, you're liable to lose both. There are things that happen to delay the locals—your grounding field disables their spark-gap engine ignition systems and often knocks out utility power. But if you then go ahead and lay a lot of additional technology on the locals to hold them back beyond that, that could escalate on you.

Once you've gotten that tough, you might as well start in with your armed landing parties, your bridge-heads, garrisons, embassies or armies of occupation or both, and the next thing you know, the Methane-Breathers want Jupiter, to "maintain the balance of power." And for what? What's the power?

*Beginning the night he wrote the XF-1000 GT story for the press kit, Jack Mullica began sleeping badly and mumbling into his pillow. A few clear sounds emerged. None were comprehensible to the average ear.

These people have nothing for us except potential. Someday, yes, they're going to be valuable, and that's why the Methane-Breathers keep hanging around, too, refilling their air tanks in the petroleum swamps at night and making funny lights when they're not careful. This is going to be a highly civilized manufacturing center someday, with factories all over the asteroid belt and on some of the bigger natural satellites, like the Moon, that'll have really significant installations. There'll be freighters and businessmen coming and going. Once you start getting that kind of traffic, you almost have to have a dockyard and maybe an actual military base—the Moon would be good for that, too—to keep a little order. There's always maintenance and repair work to be done, and there's always contraband to check for.

I keep thinking how cannabis will grow almost anywhere; one shipload of seed could make you a fortune in half a dozen places I can think of, and I don't even have a criminal mind. But the minute that kind of thing starts, you're into a commerce-regulating and immigration service kind of thing, and that's armed vehicles and men. That disturbs the Methane-Breathers, and it would disturb me if I were them. It's too easy to call a battleship just a coast guard cutter, and a regiment an inspection team. And there you go again; next thing, you've got two fleets eyeball to eyeball. And that stinks; any time you get the career armed services faced off, you're going to get actions in aid of prestige. That produces debris.

And that's apart from the fact that if the locals get on

to you and resent you, you're into a big thing with them. A slug thrower may not kill you as elegantly as a laser, but it will kill you, and these locals also have lasers. And fission and fusion and demonstrated willingness.

Then there's the fact that the tactical position of a planet-sited military force fighting off an attempted landing from space is both hopeless and unbeatable. They can't do much to you while you're aloft, but the moment you start landing they can lob all sorts of stuff at you from too many places to suppress. If you keep coming, they throw more. Pretty soon, what you're trying to land on can't be lived in. It's no good to them anymore, either, but that scores no points for you.

The same sort of thing applies if you try to destroy their military resources beforehand. At about the point where their industries might be worth taking over, locals are generally in possession of a well-dispersed, well-dug-in arsenal. That's a lot of firepower, and it takes tons more to knock out a ton of it. If we could afford to bring that much suppression to someplace out on the ass end of nowhere, we wouldn't need their damned industry in the first place.

So we don't shoot. That leaves you two alternatives. One is to poison them off—short-lived radioactives, or biologicals. Could be done, no problem with the delivery systems. Then you've got a lot of real estate, free for the burying of an entire ecological system, including the management and the work force you thought was going to sell you the produce of the factories. What you've got for your efforts is something that's turning hand over fist into a planetary desert. Thank you very much. And I, for one, would keep looking over my shoulder, and hearing whispers.

The only choice, really, is the one we make. You hang around as inconspicuously as possible, learning as much as you can from listening to and watching their electronics and so forth. You can learn a lot, by direct observation and by inference. Any intelligent race you can hope to someday relate to is going to have come up essentially the same developmental roads and dealt with the physical laws of the Universe in about the same way. So you keep tabs on them until they come out to meet you; then you can sit down right away and work things out; draw up your contracts.

If they're Methane-Breather types, of course, that's one thing; that's strictly business, and no hanging out together after working hours. If they're anthropomorphic, that's another, and welcome, brethren, into the family of spacefaring, oxygen-breathing, aspiring intelligent life, granted that's more true if it doesn't nauseate us to look at you. You also want to consider there's a lot of evidence—they say—that both the Methane-Breathers and we have found traces of some other types nosing around our corner of the Galaxy. Under those circumstances, everybody wants to be as friendly and businesslike as possible with anybody that'll have you. It could be a funny feeling to be trying to go it alone while something really exotic was undermining your back fences.

So we don't retrieve people. If something loud got

triggered off in the process, it would upset too many future arrangements. We're a pretty self-reliant kind of animal, and we also take our service oaths seriously. We knew all the possibilities before we were assigned. And besides, hardly anything ever goes wrong.

ABOUT THE CHAPLAIN

Well, sometimes you get catastrophic failures. You're working off a propulsion system that can get crosswise of a planet's magnetic field in a hurry if things go out of kilter back among the rectifiers and sorkin felkers in the mome-divider, and the most common type of failure produces a high-speed fireball that disintegrates before it hits the ground.

There was a scandal about that; some clown approved an engine design that was cheaper, easier on fuel, and, it turned out, an almost certain time bomb. It produced a mass display over the southwestern United States that they're still talking about. They claimed later they'd gotten the bugs out of it with a few modifications, but once, driving up the Merritt Parkway in Connecticut in the middle of the night, I actually saw one go up like that—brilliant and green as hell, from the copper in the hull alloy burning in contact with the air. I think they'd better put out another set of modifications.

But every so often you just hit a snag, so to speak, and that's what happened to us. So instead of working to keep you aloft at a controlled speed, the energy gets trapped inside the system and things start to soften and drip, and it gets pretty warm in the cabin.

Ravashan grunted and began hitting switches. Hanig turned up the cabin coolers and began clearing his side of the instrument board. I picked up the communicator and yelled to Selmon to hurry up and get the after bulkhead hatch shut and never mind trying to get to the engine-compartment controls. He was searing his hands on the hatch coaming; how did he expect to work the engines? With potholders? A big gob of stuff came roaring and spitting out from the blazing light beyond the hatch before he got it shut, and I put out the standard distress call.

It's all drilled into us—the entire procedure. Except for Ravashan, who had a choice between killing the engines or trying to get enough ergs out of them to land this beast, none of us had any optional moves. Unless it was the chaplain. He was staring directly back into my eyes in horror, and he was dealing with the fact that the half-molten transformer array that had come in from the engine room had hit him in the lower belly as he sat there. But none of us had the option of helping him.

I reported five men and one reconnaissance coracle with critical engine trouble over the U.S. Eastern Seaboard; took one glance at the engine temperature repeaters and added a note about no expectation of recovering control; gave the altitude, present course and speed, one crewman injured, no detectable local traffic; saw that Ravashan was heading us for the one black area in the seaboard's endless swath of light; reported that we were attempting to set down in a suggested emergency ditching area and gave its code name; and kissed my ass good-bye.

Selmon finished beating at the hatch clamps and threw himself into his chair, blowing blindly on his hands while he stared out forward over Ravashan's shoulder. I reached over and fastened his crash straps for him, and cranked our two chairs into the three-quarter angle prescribed in the hard-landing procedures manual. He and I were the two spectators. The chaplain was moaning down at his lap, which was fountaining little popping globules of flame and swirls of soot for an instant before he got to the chair-arm toggle that released his fire extinguisher, and then he was wrapped in a pressure-foamed cocoon of yellowish white gel. He looked like a monster, writhing against his straps in there.

Selmon and I watched Ravashan and Eikmo perform. I had always thought they were pretty good, for mustang officers. But I had never seen them work for their lives before. They danced fingertip ballets on their controls—Ravashan slapped Hanig's hand away from a switch at one point, never missed a beat himself, and then grabbed the copilot's wrist and guided it back to the same switch an instant later—and I knew we were going to live through it.

Even with the smoke and stink, the alarm hooter, and the wild yawing of the coracle, I had time to regret it for a moment. When you're young and you suddenly have that big block of time ahead of you to fill, drastic solutions have a certain appeal. But that's a transitory feeling that only occurs in the rational part of your mind; the animal wants to live.

Then you start worrying about being hurt in some serious way. There's only so much your survival kit can do for you. Unfortunately, from what we knew of the local culture, that was as much as their medicine could do, too. They knew how to prevent sepsis, set bones, and bypass damaged organs. And they knew immunology and antibiosis. That about summed it up. They couldn't regenerate destroyed organs and all they could do for motor nerve damage—a lacerated spinal cord, say—was to make you comfortable as much as possible.

But that was all fantasy anyway. It was a worry your mind gave you to help you ignore the possibility of outright death; it was an attempt to comfort yourself.

And then I remembered that one of us really was crippled.

It made no difference what I was thinking. Ravashan was setting us down almost as gently as a baby's kiss, sideslipping in over a bunch of scrub pines, using the cushion of some thick brush to take more of the speed off, and then down into some sort of body of shallow water hemmed in by bushes. We skipped once, snapping and drumming inside, bottomed on the mud with brown water and bits of vegetation and a smashed turtle foaming back over the viewport, swirled around in concentric spirals that threw up one last big sheet of liquid mud, and came to a crumpled stop with the radar altimeter still going ka-blip . . . ka-blip . . . ka-blip until Hanig Eikmo sighed and shut it down. The crew compartment had passed its crashworthiness test as advertised. "Well, gentlemen," Ravashan said in what I thought at the time was a pretty good American accent, "welcome to your new home."

What you want in that kind of situation is speed.

Ditching areas are preselected and coded for what we call min-time: a computer-calculated optimum average of the length of time it should take for a critical-sized team of locals to get to the impact site. Critical size is defined in numbers—three—and weight; one law-enforcement person, which is anyone in any uniform, equals three civilians. You have to assume a group of three will be able to contact reinforcements while making enough trouble to distract you, unless you act fast.

And there were other factors. There was a lot of air traffic in the area, even though the Friendship and Dulles patterns barely existed yet and even what they were then calling Idlewild was almost brand-new. They had a pretty comprehensive air traffic control system, most of it radarized, and there was military air at Atlantic City, and at Floyd Bennett and Mitchell on Long Island. I don't think McGuire AFB existed yet.

It wasn't like it would be a few years later, when the SAC and NORAD systems got into full bloom, but it was good enough; they'd seen us, for sure. They nearly always see us—our radar search receivers tell us that— but all the systems have to be designed for tracking air-breathing aircraft or ballistic missiles, and our maneuvering styles slip us off and on their screens in ways they can't really read. Still, this time it was a question of how far down they'd been able to follow us before ground return scrambled up their scopes, and how soon they'd get a search organized if they came to a decision that this time it might be worth it.

Anyway, min-time was short. We melted hell out of the controls, vaporized our charts and data storage, carved off peripheral structures and undermined the hull with lasers set at emergency overload, and tossed the guns into the bog when they got too hot to hold. They went off like small depth bombs, shattering from thermal shock as they hit the cold water.

All of that was in the procedures manual, too, and it worked like a charm. Four of us stood on some sort of clay dike overlooking a cranberry bog, with nothing but our iron rations, our survival kits, fatigue coveralls, and sweat on our faces. The guns were scattered chunks of crystal, aluminum hydroxide and copper sulfate. The pressure hull was twenty feet down, already full of silt.

The stars shone on unruffled water and four wet, muddy men full of adrenaline and ignorance.

Atop the dike, the chaplain lay wordlessly on his back. Trying to fathom his injuries, we had peeled off the gel and dropped it in the water to dissolve. Ravashan had given him some tablets of painkiller—not too many—and cut away some of his half-melted coverall below the waist. But a lot of it had amalgamated into his muscle and sinew. I remember his feet jerked constantly and his heels drummed against the ground.

I stared into Ravashan's face. Ravashan looked back at me, at Selmon, and at Eikmo. "I'll take him with me," he said.

I saw the look cross Selmon's and Eikmo's faces. How far and how long would even Ditlo Ravashan carry a dead weight?

But now we didn't have to.

The chaplain lay there, his lips moving. His name was Inava Joro, and he was about my father's age. He had done his job all during the long hours and days of our flight, keeping our heads straight, doing his best to moderate the tensions that build up among aggressive, apprehensive, finely honed young men locked up elbow to elbow in a barrel swirling toward unfriendly shores. You can't assign a woman, or even four women, to our kind of crew. That's been tried, and it turns into a zoo. And then a madhouse. So they put a little something in the food, and they do a chaplain to be a sort of umpire: a neutral party among the crew; someone who speaks and listens, and is never one of you.

I couldn't hear what he might be saying to himself. Ravashan said: "Well, Navigator?" We were running out of min-time.

I glanced up at the stars for the last time in my official capacity. A thing that's hard for locals to understand is that the constellations are composed of stars which are, generally, so far away that with a few distortions it tends to look almost the same—but wrong—from almost any planet we or the Methane-Breathers know about. When you're in flight, of course, you get the tachyon inversion effects beyond C velocity, so constellations are of purely academic interest to a navigator until he gets near dirt. But I knew enough to jerk my thumb over my shoulder. "That's west," I said, and we all said "Good luck" to each other in our native language and dispersed, each mumbling something to the chaplain as we turned our backs. Ravashan was squatted down to pick him up.

The procedures were fixed and conditioned into us. A crew must destroy what it can of its vessel and conceal the rest. Complete destruction depends on making a certain cross-connection in the engines, and that had been forestalled, but we'd done well enough. Then, after concealment, you take no artifacts with you but your rations and your survival kit, which are designed to look the way you'd expect packaged local stuff to look. On our mission, the food said Nestle's and Borden's on the wrappers, and the survival kit was a blue and white box that said Johnson & Johnson, although there wasn't any fine print and none of them were duplicates of what you'd see in a store. And then you scatter, and make every attempt to never be seen with another member of your race again.

Ravashan put the chaplain over his shoulder and moved off eastward. The chaplain's head lolled. Then he raised it briefly, and moved one arm as if he were waving.

Eikmo, Selmon, and I fanned out, the angles of our separate paths diverging, the whole nighted continent ahead of us. I moved generally westward, and after a while I couldn't hear anyone else. I heard forest noises I assumed were normal, and I heard my breathing.

You go on your own. For one thing, if the locals get on to you, you're going to be interrogated and maybe vivisected. That would put a crimp in any plans you might have for remaining in charge of your life. You can probably pass for a slightly off-brand local if you're alone; get together in a bunch, and it draws attention to little peculiarities that were going disregarded. So it's common sense, and it's in the service oath, too.

There's the catalyst phenomenon. In the Recon Service you're usually dealing with locals who are right on the brink of going off-planet. There's a good possibility you might give them technology they can replicate. Suppose some bright local figures out the principles behind one of the artifacts he drags out of your knowledge. Maybe he has some ideas of his own to add to what he learns. Then he comes up with some unique development your own people never thought of. That kind of thing can land right between your eyes, or, if they start building ships that will go faster than C, right up your family's whatsis.

By and large, it would make more sense if the services issued plain instructions to commit suicide in some way that disintegrated everything, and when you think about it, they come as close to that as they can. But if they made it an order, who would sign for it? Who'd contract-up the recon jobs? So they brief us well, drill us in the procedures, and, no doubt, hope very hard for whatever it is you'd hope for if you were in charge of the big picture.

And of course there's always your hope that you'll outlive the situation—that someday, when the papers are being signed in United Nations Plaza or Red Square or that big plot of ground in Peking, or whatever . . . well, Peking would be awkward if you didn't have the epicanthic fold around your eyes, which most of us don't . . . anyway, there'd suddenly be these two or three individuals in the surrounding crowd who'd push forward and start speaking in tongues.

But this is not a realistic hope. We don't exactly gather in new planets every year; it hasn't happened in my lifetime, and at the turn into the 1950s it seemed to me these particular people were being damned slow about qualifying.

Moon rockets don't count. That's all chemical stuff; it's like firing yourself out of a cannon. The circus crowd applauds, but it's just a piece of entertainment. Of course, Neil Armstrong and his cohorts are much braver men than I am. They have to be, to chance it in those getups. But none of us—not even poor, lonely Selmon, who actually knew something about what goes on inside a starfaring engine—is going to try to help with that.

I guess it was different in the old days here, when what you had was some finder crew stumbling into a place that was still hundreds of generations away from being ripe. It's against procedure and it's not something you'll find recognized in the official histories, but everybody knows a certain amount of hanky-panky goes on under those circumstances. The only people who'll be finders are the kind of people who'd rub themselves raw against the rules and constraints of civilization. That's why they can fly without destinations, hoping to turn up useful planets before they trip on a black hole or their toilets go into reverse. The bounty for finding a likely world is enough to suit most independent lifestyles, but sometimes there just has to be a temptation to stay and do magic for the savages.

Well, what the hell, it must be fun, being a god, and it isn't going to do a lot of harm to run off a few simple tricks for the admiring multitude in some simple corner of the world. Might even kick 'em a few steps up the ladder, though it's amazing how self-perpetuating ignorance is. Sowing a few judicious hints at that stage might even be all to the good, if it's done discreetly. But if I read the local books correctly, some of those early boys got a little out of hand. I think they attracted the fuzz and got dragged away to a reward they hadn't counted on. And it's different now; these people really are on the brink, and if I screwed things up at this critical point, you'd find my name in the books, and featured where my family and my family's friends could find it offhand. There wouldn't be much point in my going home by that route.

So we went our separate ways. I followed the dike at first, keeping my footing as best I could in the starlight. The dike and the bog terrain petered out into rising ground that was loose underfoot and difficult walking. This country was sand with a thin top layer of rotting needles and leaves. Nothing tall or sturdy could grow in it. I was constantly pulling my coveralls through underbrush and getting smeared with sap from trash pines. I wasn't sure what it was or what it might be doing to me; it smelled corrosive and felt as though it might never come off. Eventually I turned onto a crude road, keeping my eyes out for lights, listening for voices and motor noises. All I heard were insects, and I saw nothing.

The road was narrow—two ruts and a weedy strip between them. Underbrush encroached on it. It was better than the woods for forward progress, and the soil was so loose I couldn't be backtracked, so I stayed on it and didn't try to check whether I was really still headed west. I was still numb. Not much time ago, I'd been an ultracivilized man cruising airily over the patchwork lights and distorted broadcast voices of promising but unpolished folk. Now I tripped over things in the dark and wanted my mommy. I practiced my American. I said into the dark: "Any landing you can walk away from is a good landing."

NOTE ON DOTHAN STABLITS

Gouldville, in northern Indiana, is the sort of city reached by driving over railroad grade crossings. Dothan Stablits has been chief of police there since 1974, in charge of a department of about eighty-five persons, including civilian employees. In his dozen or more years of service, Chief Stablits has given the citizens of Gouldville no actionable reason to feel dissatisfied with his department, and he has been circumspect with and trustworthy to the other municipal authorities.

Stablits is a rawboned, awkwardly constituted, very large middle-aged man with a jutting jaw, slate-blue eyes, and sparse black hair. He has a tendency to stay on his feet and grip things with his gnarled hands—the back of a chair, by preference—as he speaks to visitors asking questions in his small, orderly office. He stands behind his chair, in constant incomplete motion, as if trying to find exactly the proper location to push the chair into but not sure it's not already in the right place. He chooses his words with the same sort of effect:

I was never—I never thought I'd get into enforcement work. Law enforcement. I come from Mennonite people, you know, from around Millersburg and Honeyville. Farmers; always been farmers. There's Stablitses living on their farms yet in Kutztown, Pennsylvania. There, we're *platdeutsch*—what they call Pennsylvania Dutch. We don't believe in engine-powered machinery, would you believe it, and the best job I had before I went on the cops was driving a gasoline tanker truck for Standard Oil of Indiana.

I was—I don't know, I was never the kind of person who sits down and says here I am, here's where I want to be, this is what I'll do. I've moved around a lot. I'm not the kind of person who says I don't understand it so I won't look at it, I'll never do it. A lot of us—there's just so much land, you know, and there's always a lot of brothers and sisters—there's no room on the place to feed us, a lot of us had to get jobs, and in the way it worked out, later, most of your RVs—your travel trailers and pickup truck camper inserts, your motor homes; your recreational vehicles—was Mennonite-built in factories all over this part of the state. The women would sew the curtains and make the cushions, and the men would be the cabinetmakers and body builders. And every once in a while, when the elders weren't looking, some of the younger men would run a forklift in the lumber shed or actually go out on the road with a unit for a test run. Well, you know, you do that kind of thing when you're young. Then you get older. I think maybe most of the elders know all about that. They see but they don't say, because they know everybody gets older.

I was—well, I was taken with this one girl. And she went to Chicago; her aunt there died, and her uncle needed somebody to cook and clean, he was old. I went and looked for work up there so I could live and call on her. Well, the uncle died and it came out at the wake she was expecting.

Then she had—she got the idea to be a barmaid. There are people who will get into that because they can sleep while the kid is in the day-care and work while the kid is sleeping. And there are then people who will like that kind of life, and I have never seen one of those change away from it until they got too crippled up for the action. So I went on the Chicago PD with a fellow I met delivering gasoline in the middle of the night. But that was no work for me, it was in the Summerdale District, maybe you heard about that, and I quit there before that burglar testified and it all blew up. I went to Shoreview, the next town, because they were making a lot of sergeants up there fast and I liked the work, basically. I still like it. It's good.

I, well, I was getting along, and this guy went down on the CTA tracks. I have to tell you, I worried about that. But I couldn't handle—I couldn't get a handle on it. There was—well, look, it's not like Sherlock

Holmes. I have never seen a case solved yet by adding up all the clues and dividing by logic. You don't say "solved." You say "cleared." You don't say "clue." You say "lead"—you get a lead to somebody who saw something, or heard something, and you get that person to tell you what they saw or heard in such a way that it gives you the next lead. And I couldn't get any. But— but I knew—I know to this day—there're leads out there somewhere.

Are you trying to tell me the man fell? Then he fell when there were still people around who had been on the train with him. If they were within a hundred yards, they must have seen something; I mean, there's a flash, and there's noise. Where are they? Or else he waited until they were a ways off.

Do you want me to think he was a jumper? What the dickens did he go all the way up to Borrow Street to jump for? Was he trying to leave a message for somebody lived around there—see what you made me do? Then where is that person?

Was he pushed? Then that person knows what happened. He remembers. He could tell me. Or he could tell somebody. You don't forget a thing like that; it lives in you. It makes you move in ways different from the way you'd move if it had never happened. Little ways, maybe, at first. But they add up, and someday you put your feet entirely different from how you would have if you hadn't pushed him. And that will be a lead. Anybody knows me, knows I can wait a long time for a lead.

At this point, Chief Stablits shrugs and looks around his office as if discovering it was some other room; his arms rise and fall, his hands slap his thighs.

But there's just so long you can keep a file active when your commander says it was just some guy on the tracks, it wasn't dope or bets or the Mafia; it's not something the city manager's going to feel heat, the town's going to the dogs, do something. And there's just so much time in a day, and sometimes these things can take years . . . well, a lot of them never come to anything, really—you can't be sure, they could just as lief pop open on you, I have to admit that. But you can't hang your hat on it. And one day there's a letter from here, from Gouldville, it's the town council, they say they're looking for a new chief and I've been recommended. Well, there's the pay, and there's the being the commander, and, tell you the truth, there's the getting away from the man on the tracks and all the other open files. So I came here and talked to them, and I got hired.

Do I wonder how they got my name, in particular? You mean, why would they write to a sergeant in Shoreview, in particular? No, there's nothing to wonder about that. They had a list made up by this company, and I was on it, that's all. Yeah, it took me off that case; it took me off a lot of cases.

He pushes the chair to a new place and shortly thereafter the interview is over.

Stablits's name did, indeed, appear on a list prepared by an employment search agency specializing in municipal positions. A similar list was furnished to a number of other communities within reasonable distance of Shoreview. The list was accompanied by brief dossiers on the subject individuals. It was sent to every community with a high-rank opening in its police department, and Stablits's is the best dossier in every instance. It is also the only one common to all the lists, which contained no other duplications. I have been able to establish this much by examination of records stored by those municipalities.

The lists were volunteered. The firm had not been contacted, but apparently had some means of compiling a roster of openings. The firm was not one of the leading agencies specializing in this sort of work, and has long since gone out of business without a trace. And therefore there is no way to tie it back to whoever is behind the National Register of Pathological Anomalies.

—A.B.

DITLO RAVASHAN'S STATEMENT ON EVENTS IMMEDIATELY FOLLOWING THE CRASH

I am Ditlo Ravashan. On the night in question, I succeeded in making a forced landing in the New Jersey cranberry swamps. With me were Hanig Eikmo, Olir Selmon, Dwuord Arvan and Inava Joro. Joro was severely wounded by the breakup of the engine; the others sustained no wounds.

After we had disposed of the ship, we set out in different directions and I did not ever see my crewmen again. I carried Joro for a time, but he was getting worse and worse despite everything I could do for him, and shortly he died.

I buried the body deep, and not even I could find it again. It has never been found. I managed to reach a highway, and in due course was able to hitch a ride to Atlantic City Naval Air Station, where I entered the service of the United States, to which I have been completely loyal from that day to this.

This is a true and accurate account, and it is complete.

—Ditlo Ravashan

A TRUE AND ACCURATE, COMPLETE ACCOUNT BY DITLO RAVASHAN FOR HIS OWN FILES

Unlike the others, I had an exact idea of where I was, and a fair outline of what I would do if possible. I waited until the other three had gotten over their first confusion, waiting as usual with perfect patience since it cost me nothing, and after a time the three of them set out in different directions, as they had been taught.

Once we had parted company, I moved off in the direction of a two-lane highway, carrying Joro for a time. I remember that except for Joro's incessant moaning the night was still and clear. "I don't—don't think I can—stand the pain!" he said at one point. What did he expect that to do—make the pain go away? In truth, I was sick and tired of him since considerably before the crash. I would certainly have left him—would have never picked him up in the first place—but he was needful for my plan, and so I carried him patiently. But after a time I laid him down, for his gasps had grown both more frequent and more shallow, and it was obvious that soon I would be alone.

Joro lay staring blindly up at me, his hands hugging his belly. "What's going to become of me?" he asked.

"Chaplain," I said, "you're going to die. If I had all of a military hospital here to help, I think you'd still die. And that's the truth."

"But I don't want to—"

"Chaplain, you have the choice between going down a whimpering, puling babe, or dying like a man. That's your only choice."

"Oh, Ravashan, why—why did we come all this way?"

"Chaplain, we really don't have time for this. Be useful. There is a question I hope you can answer."

"Wh-what do you want to know?"

"What is the meaning of life?"

"Wh—" He did not answer at first, so I struck him lightly in the face.

"Chaplain Joro."

He stopped his moaning, but did not otherwise respond. I struck him a little harder. "Chaplain. Answer the question."

Joro looked at me, and it seemed some sort of remission were temporarily taking place, for his breathing steadied for a moment. "Ravashan," Joro said. "You're crazy."

"Chaplain, there is nothing I or anyone else can do for you. You *are* dying. Tell me, if you can, the meaning of life." I struck him again, but all he did was weep.

"Ssss . . ." His eyes had closed and his head drooped. I struck him again.

"Chaplain—what *is* the meaning of life? Do you hear me? What is the meaning of life?" I crouched over him in the darkness, repeating the question tirelessly, but all he said was "Hurt—" and then he lapsed into incoherent gibberish until he died.

Somehow, the night did seem a little more alien with him gone, for a moment or two. But I was . . . buttering no parsnips . . . where I was, and I wanted to be far away from the swamp by the time dawn occurred. So I shouldered my burden—it was a dead weight now, but on the other hand it was quiet—and in due course found the highway, a clear cut through the countryside, with soft sand shoulders. There was no appreciable light, but there were stars, and by the starlight I could tell that I had happened upon country in transition from the bogs and trees to bullrushes. I was not really near the coast, as yet, but I could expect estuaries, and creeks running to meet them.

The highway was deserted. Well, at that time of the morning it would be, for the most part. But somebody was bound to come along. I set Joro down on the shoulder and waited.

I remember what I thought. Two things, leading up to a third:

From time to time, birds went by overhead, on their own errands. Birds as such were not known on my home world, though they were on some others—including this one, obviously. We had, instead, creatures that navigated the air using the displacement of their bodies, distended by digestive gases. These were capable of a slow sort of dirigibility, enough to eat seeds and insects, and at the higher end of the chain, predatory types that ate lesser flying creatures. So they served the same purpose.

I have heard it said that the lack of birds on my home world can be explained by the fact that birds are actually descended from dinosaurs, or the equivalent. And dinosaurs, or the equivalent, were unknown to my people's paleontology. The theory is that *we* are the dinosaurs— that in due course, we shall devolve into birds. So I followed the flight of these Terrestrial birds with some interest.

I watched the man-made air traffic, too, wondering if they were attempting a search for us. But I noticed nothing concentrating on the swamp. In fact, I noticed nothing out of the ordinary: propeller planes, almost exclusively, and mostly commercial, judging by their height and size. One or two jets went by overhead; those were military, but none of them showed any interest in my particular part of the darkness below them.

And the upshot of these thoughts, for what it's worth, was that this was a relatively primitive world, and so I was comparatively safe from anything the natives might do. And at the same time it was a world sufficiently advanced for me to enjoy myself upon it. I was not at all sure that I would have been as happy on my own world, all things considered. There were quite a few Ditlo Ravashans back there. Here there was only one, and I was he, and this planet would support me in the style to which I intended to become accustomed. It was not an unpleasant thought.

After a while, the lights of a car began to glow in the distance, and I stepped out into the road. I reckoned that a uniformed man, which I was, so soon after the war, in trouble—which I was—would be able to flag down most forms of transportation. I was almost wrong, as it turned out. The car swerved and slid, and almost made it around me, in which case it might have sped up again and gone, but in the end it did stop, and the driver rolled down his window and poked a pale and bewildered face at me. "Wha-what do you want?" he said in a breathless and slightly drunken voice.

He was a middle-aged man, with his tie undone, who was probably returning home to wife and children after a night partly spent with another woman. There was a smell to him of cheap perfume, and there was lipstick on his left ear. And he could not make up his mind about me, as I suspected he could not make up his mind about many other things as well.

I said, as he looked at me with his mouth slightly open and his eyes trying for sharper focus: "Get me to Atlantic City Naval Air Station as fast as you can. My buddy's hurt bad." I said it just like that, and if my accent wasn't quite right, my uniform wasn't, either; it was just a coverall with a couple of badges sewn on. But I didn't expect either one of these things to give me trouble with this man, and they didn't.

He demurred only about the destination. He looked

for a moment at Joro, lying huddled on the shoulder, a dim figure in the backscatter from the headlights, and said, "But there's lots of places closer than Atlantic City."

Not with military personnel. Not that I knew of. "Atlantic City is where we have to go."

"Well, all right, I was just—" But I was gone away from his window, opening his offside door, wrestling Joro into the backseat, and settled in beside the driver, before he could complete the thought. And if he was a little amazed at how fast I did all that, he did not speak of it. He craned his neck to look at Joro again, and I said, "Let's go."

He nodded uncertainly, but put the car in gear, and began climbing up the ladder of speeds until he had the car up to highway velocity. "You got it," he said, having decided that, really, it was all his idea.

It was too much to hope, of course, that the Earthman would just drive and do his job. He was a man who thought of himself as being different from other men because he had a woman on the side, and he was a man who, underneath that, realized that he was overweight and over age and not especially lovely to look at, so that some small but vital part of ·him knew that his woman on the side was either desperate or playing him for a fool, or perhaps both, and therefore he actually got no pleasure from his pleasure. So every opportunity to open up his life, to give it meaning and texture, was, necessarily, exploited. So about ten minutes into it, he began talking. "Can't get much more than seventy out of this bucket without goin' all over the road," and "Boy! Have I got a story to tell my wife!" and similar expressions. Well, Joro wasn't in any kind of a rush, actually. As for the Earthman's wife, whatever he told her wasn't going to be believed. "Your buddy doesn't look too good, what I could see of him. What kind of outfit you in?" was closer to the mark.

"Brazilian Naval Air Force," I said. "We're allies of yours. Night flying exercise. Couple of things went wrong."

"Oh." There was a pause. "Hadn't you better check on your buddy?"

"My buddy's as all right as he needs to be."

"Oh." More thought. "What about your plane?"

"I know where it is. The naval station will send out a recovery vehicle, have it back at the air station by dawn."

"Oh." I could see him pondering that. The next thing out of his mouth might be *You know, there's something fishy about this story*, so I said: "Sooner we get to the authorities, the better," and he remembered that we were, after all, headed for the authorities. Which meant, I suppose, that no matter how fishy the story, it had the official sanction of the United States government; which meant, since he was too clever to be taken in by it but it was the story the government wanted told, that he could tell the story without feeling like a fool, and with the feeling he was on the inside of something.

It never occurred to him, I reckon, that somebody would head to the authorities who didn't belong to the authorities.

We pulled up, finally, at the main gate of the naval air station. It was before you actually got to Atlantic City, on the highway that ran through the cattails, and though it was off to one side it was easy enough to direct him to it . . . it was, really, the only thing that looked like a naval station, and one of the few things that were lit up at night.

The gate was a guard shack with the highway dividing to run to either side, and two guards in it, except that they came out, carrying rifles, as the car came toward them but then turned partway to go back, and yet stopped. The guards looked at us . . . like we had two heads . . . and they pointed their weapons at us.

I reached into the backseat and pulled Joro out. Rigor had set in; he was like a wooden dummy, and very cold to the touch, even though he was at the ambient air temperature or even above it. He sprawled on the tarmac, one leg in the air, hands over his belly, and this was the first I'd seen him that way in the light; he was dirty, pieces of foam clung to him, pieces of coverall were blended with scorched flesh, and his mouth was ruined.

The guards were not combat veterans. One of them choked down an outcry. The other reacted to the thump of Joro's body on the tarmac by firing his rifle automatically; that was how I learned the weapons weren't loaded, for all I heard was the click of the firing pin. I turned to the driver of the car. "You can go now." And he did, with one glance at Joro, sick dismay beginning to dawn on his face, backing the car until he could complete turning it around and go, where the first thing he would have to explain to his wife would be the lipstick, which would mean he might never have to explain anything else. I turned to the guards, who were very young. "Let me speak to your commanding officer," I said, and let the military routine take over.

There was a great deal to it, of course, and I did not speak to the commanding officer until I had worked my way up the chain of command. But eventually I spoke to an adjutant, and explained that Joro's body wasn't getting any sweeter-smelling, and at that stage they put it on ice somewhere. And then I did get to speak to the commanding officer, and explained to him that what he was wanted for was to relay my demand to speak to a government official.

And by then there was enough mystery about me, what with my uniform badges that looked real only at first glance, and my first-aid kit, which had Johnson & Johnson on it but just wavy lines where smaller letters should go, and only slightly comprehensible things inside, and as luck would have it, spending the night at the naval station was a young congressman who until recently had been in the Navy. They got him up; in truth, he undoubtedly was up by then, and possibly even had had breakfast, but they told me they got him up, and they brought him to my room, with a couple of really armed guards to keep him safe. And so this man who was to be wedded to me in so many ways over the years to come came into the gray room where I sat. He looked at me, and sat down in a chair opposite mine, across the plywood table. He cocked his head and watched me. He did not, at first, speak.

I explained about Joro's body—that it would require a confidential autopsy which would prove my bona fides. The congressman nodded—he was quick, and that was far from the last time he would display that quality—and waved the military personnel out of the room, although they were very uncomfortable with that. I could hardly blame them, but the congressman was right—he was utterly safe from me, because he was the key to what I wanted.

I told him what I was. And he believed me. And we worked out a deal, which has been very good for me and not bad for the congressman, either. An early part of the deal, as we worked it out across the plywood table, was that he would call me by a nickname, and I would call him by a nickname, and avoid what might happen if our real names became known at some time. It was only the first of myriad precautions we would take, in the end. It has been so long, now, that I have trouble thinking of him as anyone but Yankee. And I think that is for the best.

—Never revealed.

HANIG EIKMO, Part One

Retracing Hanig Eikmo's path has not been easy. Not because it was so complicated but because it was so simple. Hanig seemed to be a man of direct action, a man who would solve problems characteristically with his hands, not with his mind. Therefore, it became at times infuriatingly difficult to reason out what he would have done next, because what he did next was often spur-of-the-moment.

Too, he was by far the weakest speaker of American, barely advanced beyond the mandatory classes at the trade school he went to instead of the Academy, and barely having learned any more from the radio and television during the trip. He seemed uninterested in most things, even things almost anyone else would have thought vital. Therefore, he did not interact as much with Americans as his fellow crewmen did, and tended to live by himself. This was particularly true during the early years of his exile, but it was always true to a large extent.

But in the end it did not matter, as it turns out. But I am getting well ahead of myself. Best to tell Hanig's story simply as it unfolded, for him, to the best of my ability to reconstruct it.

After the crew split up, Hanig went on through the night, very steadily, looking little to the left or right, until he came, in due course, to a creek. There he stopped long enough to put a hand in the water. Determining in which direction the water was running, he proceeded along the bank, downstream. And again in due course, he came to an estuary. Technically, it was a river, for the creek emptied into it, but the water was plainly salt when he tasted it; the tide came up this far. And now he had a choice to make.

At this point, he would leave solid ground; the cattails grew on either side from a base of water, the soil that nourished them being submerged. But it was not a real choice. To stay with relatively firm footing, he would have to divert, and divert into a land of which he knew very little. If he stayed with the estuary, he was in much more familiar territory, for his youth had been spent in country much like this. A little testing showed that he could follow the water at least for a time without having it close over his head, so he proceeded to do that. And though in time the water did become too deep for literal wading, it was calm, so that he was able to half swim, half gain a foothold and jump forward in the water, and continue to move downstream at a good pace.

A more cautious person might have given thought to marine denizens of various kinds—the more trouble-some because largely unknown to Eikmo. But as it happens, with the exception of sharks—which did not normally penetrate this far inland, and, if they did, were only liable to attack under the most extraordinary circumstances—Eikmo had in a manner of speaking picked a climatic range in which the water was free of that. Farther south he would not have been as lucky, but he was not farther south. He made his way through the night, taking as much care as practical to keep rea-sonably quiet, and that was that.

And in due course he came upon a sailboat, tied up to the dock/veranda of a shack built on stilts. It was a bit of a shock; one moment he was moving onward, with nothing to either side but the dim shadows of cattails, and the next he had rounded a turn and found this. But he was not truly surprised. In fact, he had been looking for it, and considered that it was only a matter of time until he made his way close enough to the sea to come upon the home of a waterman.

There were no lights—not in the shack, not on the boat, not even running lights. Levering himself out of the water onto the dock, he listened. There was someone sleeping in the shack, but that did not immediately dis-turb Eikmo. He slipped aboard the boat, a twenty-four-foot yawl, and found it perfect; certainly showing signs of wear and tear, but the sails were apparently whole, being loosely gathered at the base of the mast with a few turns of cordage to keep them so, and the hull was sound. With that learned, he examined the ties to the dock and found that one of them was a padlocked chain, despite the fact that access to shack and boat was limited to water. He examined the chain and found it strong, and fastened to an eyebolt through the dock, the other end of the eyebolt with its threads apparently damaged deliberately so that the nut could not be backed off—at least not by Eikmo's hand. Shaking his head, he now entered the shack and stood over the sleeping occupant.

The interior of the shack was dim, and he could not make out much detail, but it was one room, plus the veranda/dock from which, undoubtedly, the occupant fished from time to time, and the occupant was alone. He was a man of thirty or so, who had gone to sleep with his clothes largely on, and judging by the smell which fountained up from his mouth—he was on his back—he had gone to sleep drunk. Eikmo killed him swiftly, by breaking his neck, and searched his clothes until he found the key to the padlock.

He now had transportation. It did not take long to puzzle out the mysteries of the yawl rig. In a matter of several hours, he was down through the increasingly broad estuaries and on the ocean, and then around Cape May into Delaware Bay. Full daylight saw him headed in the general direction of Dover, Delaware.

The bay was not, even then, the loveliest of spots; the water that sometimes literally foamed back from the hull was liberally laced with chemicals and detergents, and yellowish; nor was it helped by Eikmo's having to tack, again and again, against a quartering breeze. But he forged on, ducking the tankers and freighters that occasionally cut across his path.

In due course, he found a landfall in the form of a long, deserted, weather-beaten dock poking out into the bay, flanked by an obviously abandoned building and some distance from a highway he could see. That was the extent of civilization at this point, Dover being inland by a few miles, but for Eikmo the highway was the important thing, with its traffic proceeding more from left to right than from right to left.

He scrambled onto the dock, taking a few things with him and lashing the wheel of the boat. He watched the boat start to sail away, and then he turned shoreward. He made his way over some broken concrete and then through a scrub field to the shoulder of the highway, which was the main coastal artery but was two-lane, if concrete. He studied the traffic flow, and then he began to walk in the direction of Dover. In due course the highway became a street. And so he proceeded, gradually seeing signs of life in the form of decaying houses and stores, and then somewhat less decayed structures, and the occasional human, and being passed by cars, and in a little while he was walking down an undoubted human street in an undoubted human city, with humans here and there, and he betraying no sign that he was any different from them or did not belong there.

He had, aside from his iron rations and his first-aid

kit, a compass, a chronometer, and a portable marine band radio. He had also changed from his uniform into paint-spattered jeans and a T-shirt, which, though somewhat skimpy for the weather, and short, were of course far safer than his uniform. The latter was at the bottom of the bay.

He found a pawnshop in due course, probably simply going along until he came to a store window full of all sorts of things with only portability in common. But remember that he had the items in the first place; he knew there was someplace where you could get money for items without clear title. True, he traded in the stolen goods for a very little amount of money—he could not bargain, of course, though I doubt he would have even if fluent in American—and with that little bit of money bought some clothes at a secondhand store; a better-fitting pair of jeans, and much cleaner; and the same for a T-shirt, which he topped with a blue chambray shirt and a pea coat. He kept his issue socks, underwear, and shoes. In fact, he still had the shoes, years later, and though they were like no pair on Earth at the time, neither were they outlandish, and he saw no point in discarding them. (It is also possible he wanted something to tie him back to the world of his birth.)

Outfitted, so to speak, he next waited beside one of several saloons, and, picking his victim judiciously, relieved a sailor of his pay, which came to several hundred dollars. He killed again, yes.

With that much for a stake, he moved to the Greyhound station, where he bought a ticket to Denver . . .

quite possibly because it was the easiest city name to pronounce. Practically every city name has a variety of possible pronunciations, except Denver. And in due course he arrived there.

In Denver he lived for many years, working as a day laborer, getting paid at the end of each day, sleeping in flophouses and eating in diners, distinguished from his fellow denizens only in that he did not drink. He really seems to have been content with his lot, and if he hadn't accidentally seen Ravashan on a stopover on his way to Colorado Springs, he might be there yet, and reasonably happy, and out of this story entirely.

But he is not out of it.

—A.B.

JACK MULLICA

The sand road gradually widened and became firmer. I was conscious of piled trees, and clear-cut patches in the growth. Apparently someone intended, or had intended, some form of enterprise here. Whether it still proceeded, during the day, or not, I had no idea. But certainly it was abandoned by night.

I came to a road bridge—concrete, as I later confirmed—lichened, partially eroded away, but still sound enough. It was not very long. An enameled sign, very worn, proclaimed MULLICA RIVER, and, in truth, there was some water in the bed below, but if this was a river, it was a poor excuse for one. And in any case the road kept on going, a track through the quiet and the darkness, until finally up ahead I could hear something. I stopped.

I strained to hear anything that would give me a clue

to what lay ahead. But none of it made sense to me. There was something that sounded like muffled laughter, and the sound of glass on glass, but I could make nothing of that. I stood for a while in the darkness, and then I moved forward, toward the sounds, very slowly.

Gradually, they grew clearer; they were the sound of two or three males, drinking and carousing. They were also the sound of one female, and though at first hers had blended in with the male voices, now it was in an increasingly different tone: less companionable, more argumentative. And the male voices grew less festive.

I moved forward again, and now I could see the shadowed form of a parked car, and cigarettes, and increasingly tense voices. "Goddamn, Margery, what the hell?" suddenly came clear.

"I want to go home," said the woman.

"Margery, we ain't through here."

"Yes, we are. I have to get up early in the morning and work. You've had all the fun you're going to have for one night."

There was a giggle, and a different male voice said: "*I* ain't so sure about that. How 'bout the rest of you fellers?"

Margery's voice was suddenly cold. "The only way you're going to get more is to commit rape. And if you do that, you'd better kill me afterward."

"Rape!" The voice was incredulous; it was the giggler. "Rape!" But the other males were more thoughtful. And just as cold; one of them, the leader, I suppose, said:

"All right, Margery," in a calm voice. "All right." And suddenly the back door of the car flew open, and for a moment there was light, so that I could see the woman come tumbling out, to fall heavily to the ground, grunting. "All right, Margery. And good night." The door closed and the light went out. The car started and the headlights flicked on. "Enjoy the walk home." And the car pulled away, all revelry gone, and in a little while it was dark again except for the starlight, and I could hear Margery cursing softly as she got to her feet and stood in the road, looking after it.

She didn't know I was there only a few steps away. She moved, an awkward, twisting motion, and it was obvious to me that she'd been hurt by her fall. And she began to walk up the road, each step slow and unbalanced; she was limping badly.

"Miss?"

"Holy Jesus, Mary, and Joseph! Who the hell is that?"

"Jack," I said, taking the name of the all-American boy. "Jack . . . Mullica. I was walking along a minute ago, and I saw—"

"Jesus H. Christ! You were walking along?"

"That's right. And I—"

"You scared the shit out of me!"

"Well, I'm sorry. Look, can I help you? You look like you're walking hurt. I've got a first-aid kit, and—"

Her sudden chuckle was both amused and bitter. "It'll take more than first aid to help that. A lot more."

I didn't understand. But that was not as important as

reaching some sort of accommodation with her. "Well, look, whatever you say—will it help you to lean on me as we walk?"

Her chuckle this time was rueful, and still bitter but not as much. "Yes, it will help. Especially considering that we have over two miles to go. Bastards. All right—come on." She moved over next to me, on the left. She was almost as tall as I. I noticed that she smelled of perfume—some artificial scent. And we began to walk along the road through the dark, slowly and, for her, painfully. But she settled in against my hip, and I thought to myself, abruptly, about her as a woman, not as an Earth person, and I didn't know what to make of that, but it was better than not thinking of her as a woman.

She asked, almost immediately: "Where'd you come from?"

"I got lost," I said at once, having anticipated that I would have to account for myself to someone. "I was hitching a ride, and they let me out in the dark, and I got lost."

"Uh-huh. And what kind of an accent is that?"

"Indian. East Indian."

"Uh-huh." She seemed disinclined to pursue this line any further. We walked along in silence for a while. Then she said: "I don't suppose you have a place to stay."

"Well, no."

"Yeah. All right—you can stay with my father and me, for a while. Sleep in the barn."

I thought that over. "All right. Thank you; it's kind of you."

"You're helping me get home. Helping a lot. This leg of mine hasn't been good for much since I was a little girl. Polio. So it's a fair exchange." Her voice was flat—there was not a trace of her feeling sorry for herself. But, of course, she'd had time to prepare the statement. "My name's Margery Olchuk, by the way. And yours is Jack Mullica." Again, her voice was flat.

"That's right. Jack Mullica."

"All right." And after that she concentrated on walking. Even with me to help her, it was no picnic for her.

> —Reconstruction, as best as possible, of various bits and snatches Mullica mouthed in his sleep

OPENING STATEMENT BY YANKEE

The Navy man shaking me by my shoulder and saying my name over and over was apologetic. And he was very cautious: "We have a man here who turned up in the middle of the night. We don't know who he is. The C.O. thinks we should wake you." And he retreated across the room while I woke.

And awake I did, slowly—that is, externally I was slow. But I was processing the information quite rapidly. Paramount was the fact that instead of handling it routinely, the C.O. was awakening me. So the odds were overwhelming that the man was not mental; the odds were overwhelming that the C.O. at least felt that with a member of Congress on the base, he had to include him in whatever it was, or risk censure for not having done so. That made it serious. So I woke up slowly, but by the time my feet hit the deck, I was ready for anything.

After a quick shower and hasty breakfast, I followed the Navy man to the door of the mystery man's room, where we were met by an armed party. After my nod, we went in.

The man seated there had a definite air about him. He was dark, handsome in a hawkish way, dressed in some sort of fatigue uniform, and as he stood up I saw that he was tall. He extended his hand. "Hello." His voice was almost accentless, but a little stiff, as though he were first thinking out his phrases in some other language. "My name is Ditlo Ravashan. Captain Ravashan, I think you would say, except that I have no vessel any longer." He said that, and then he smiled.

I studied his hand. Then I took it, and as I took it, I felt for the first time the incredible power of the man. It was as if steel—warm steel—had closed around me. If he did not want to give my hand back, I simply could not take it. But he gave it back.

I looked at him. And I knew—I don't know how, but I *knew*—what he would claim about his origins. I gave him my name and my position in the U.S. Congress, while looking directly into his eyes. They were brown, and there was little to see that was different, though they tended more toward the maroon than was common in a white man. And they were as steady as mine. And he grinned suddenly, a sharp broadening of his smile into something else entirely. "You've guessed," he said approvingly. "You've actually guessed! From very small clues indeed! Bravo! But to remove any lingering doubts," he said, "I brought in a body—another of my crew. It won't take much cutting to determine we are different from you, inside."

"No, I don't doubt you," I said, making up my mind. If it was true about having a body, there was no longer any doubt. He'd brought it to us to spare the need for cutting him. I could hardly blame him. "All right—leave us alone," I said to the Navy party. "All of you," to the C.O. It wasn't that I didn't trust them. It was a matter of need to know, that's all. And they went, although the C.O. was frowning and hesitating. A better man would have stayed, but the better man had been discharged after the end of the war.

Ravashan and I looked at each other across the room. Then we sat down on opposite sides of the table. "What do you want, Ravashan?"

Ravashan grinned. "Don't you want to know how I got here, where my ship is, and so forth?"

"I'll learn all that, in time," I said. "You obviously didn't plan it; you're improvising. That's the primary fact."

Ravashan sat silently for a moment, looking at me. And in that look, I read him for what he was—an uncommonly clever individual, sizing me up, and not realizing that I was more clever than he. And he *was* clever—far cleverer than any man I knew, in his situation. I respected him for that. More important, I prepared to enjoy our association, and he did not disappoint me for a long time.

He began to speak; of long voyages, at first:

"We range," he said, "over a fair part of the immediate Universe. Well, we should—we've been at it for a long time. Long time. You have got to understand that, nevertheless, we haven't even scratched the surface of the stars in this immediate vicinity. There are very many of them. But in those stars, we have found only one race that was in space before us. Those are the Methane-Breathers. We . . . traffic . . . with them. We are not enemies. But we are not friends, either. If we had an interest in the same worlds, I think we would be deadly enemies. But never mind that for now.

"We explore the stars for many reasons, but the main one is commerce. Natural resources. And the occasional customer."

"Oh?" I said.

He laughed. "We have, as you can imagine, things for sale. Machinery, technology packages, even gadgets. All, of course, more advanced that anything your race possesses. In return, we take a certain spectrum of natural resources. Sometimes, too, we find articles of native manufacture for which there is a market . . . much as your more advanced nations will buy certain goods from less advantaged cultures, because they are cheaper for the disadvantaged to make, or because the goods are somehow cute. I'm sure you know what I mean."

"Yes." But I barely noticed the insult. Why should I? I had already established that I was more intelligent than he. What was important was his talk of advanced machinery and consumer goods. True, they would collapse the domestic manufacturing capability if introduced at random. But they did not have to be introduced at random, if one were careful. And the man who controlled the flow . . . the man who controlled the flow would become the most powerful man on Earth. The most powerful man on Earth. But all I said was "Yes."

He said: "There's a catch, unfortunately."

"And what is that?"

"It's illegal. Even my telling you this is illegal. We take an oath. We are not, under any circumstances, to communicate the truth of ourselves to the natives. We are not for a moment to even consider it. It's too soon in your development."

I looked at him. He looked back. I said: "Why, then, are you breaking your oath?"

"Well, wouldn't you? If you were me, and faced years of a wasted life now?" He took a breath. "When I obviously was born to engage life?"

I grinned mirthlessly. In some ways, we were very much alike. He went on: "So I need protection not only from your people but from mine. Oh, not for a while. But if we are to do each other any good, then in time I may have advanced the Earth to the point where an official commercial envoy lands. And at that point, I had better not be the individual who took so many risks with the secret of our existence." He grinned wryly. "Precisely because I would have gotten away with it. That they dare not forgive."

I stopped him then and called the C.O. I could not, of course, exercise any duress over the commanding officer, and I could not keep him from informing his

superiors . . . in fact, he had so informed them even
before waking me. What he had informed them of was
that he had an unaccounted-for personnel who had told
a good enough story to get on the base . . . with a
corpse. That had been enough for the Navy to send a
specialist, who was on his way and would arrive shortly,
and depending on what the specialist recommended,
further action would be taken. Presumably, that included giving the C.O. a discharge if he had pulled the
wrong chain frivolously. Well, that was right, proper,
and did not perturb me—though it obviously perturbed
the C.O. I did not think the story that this man might
be from off Earth had gotten beyond the confines of the
base as yet, and even on the base the number of persons
who knew even a wildly distorted version was minimal.

Furthermore, I did not know if an un-Earthling had
ever previously been encountered, but that did not mean
much; you can trust any branch of the service above a
certain level of rank to keep its secrets. But a secret
like this had the quality that, except in very special
circumstances, it could be bandied about and still it was
too huge to be believed.

What I wanted to make sure of, nevertheless, was
that all the enlisted men were not in communication
with the news media. Enlisted men have an almost
unique ability to make trouble, in a clumsy, sloppy way
that is almost impossible to deny because you can't be
sure what it is about, so muddled does it become. And
as for the news media—even in those early days I regarded it with suspicion on the one hand and contempt

for its manipulability on the other. And, as I rather thought, the C.O. had secured the base, and would only gradually release the men who had seen or heard anything, transferring one to Alaska and one to Hawaii, one to Norfolk, and so forth. And really, what did they know; what hard facts did they possess? Good. With that assurance, I dismissed the C.O. and returned to my un-Earthly man.

We reasoned on what sort of questions the investigating officer would ask when he got there, and how my man would respond. And also I thought it likely I foresaw what I would do next. So that was that.

Ravashan would be loyal to me, I thought, above all other things on Earth . . . and for that matter, when push came to shove, above all things off Earth, too, though I did not make that clear to him. I did not at once know exactly how he could best serve me. But serve me he would. Plainly he was too precious to let slip away, and I could always think of something later. And so, in that room, the two of us struck a bargain that endured for many years. It did not, of course, endure forever. But nothing is forever.

—From a private tape

OLIR SELMON

I was terrified. Every noise of the night seemed monstrous. I saw nothing in the dark; I collided with a hundred things in the first five minutes, and to this day I can only guess at what they were.

I blundered on. And as I blundered, I went through the first of what I would go to sleep with every night for the rest of my life. I conducted an enquiry: *Why* did the engines suddenly begin to fail? *What* did I do wrong in attempting to restore the balance? *When* had they actually begun to fail . . . was it, for instance, as soon as we started them up at home? Had they *never* actually been right, and I, fool, had not noticed? Had we in fact been lucky to reach this planet at all, before the trouble became too catastrophic? Could I, in short, have done *anything* differently; and if I had, would it have made a difference? I could not know . . . all my life I would continue to ask these questions.

And I tried to convince myself that in fact it had not happened—that I was sleeping aboard the ship, and would waken at any time now, and shake my head ruefully, and go on about my duties, safe and sound. But I was not safe and sound, and I knew it.

I blundered on. And on. It seemed to me that I would never get out of this trackless maze of sharp objects in the dark, of unknown voices crying who knew what, in response to what, with the object of what. And *why* did the engines fail? And Joro. Poor, luckless Joro.

It was dawn, gradually filtering through the trees, that brought a measure of a sort of calm. First of all, I could see the trees, at last, and pick my way among them, so that the innumerable bristlings of branchlets and twigstickers lessened to almost nothing. I was bleeding, lightly, from a hundredfold pervasions of my skin, and my coverall was punctured and stained with blood and sap, but all of me was functioning, and with dawn the quality of noises, too, went through a diminishment, so I found that I was clearly less nervous, and that, too, helped calm me. But what was I to do? Where was I to go?

Indeed, my options seemed so few. So very few. Here I was, stranded for life, with nothing beyond what I could carry, and who would give me shelter, who would give me a place of livement, when the situation would produce questions I could not answer? What was I to do? Where was I to go? And, asking myself these questions, I moved on, with neither plan nor direction, with no purpose beyond sheer survival, and what good, really, was that?

I confess it freely—if I had had a weapon, at certain points on that first morning, I would have, indeed, turned it on myself . . . if I could have thought of a way to do so and yet conceal the weapon after my death. It is good that doctrine does not allow us to salvage weapons, for surely a weak being might not, in the last extremity of despair and spiritual debility, take as much care for the last part as he should, and would leave a mysterious and rankling corpse, and beside it a weapon of great puissance and intrigue; it was good that the doctrine did not permit us to salvage weapons, I repeated to myself, and sobbed.

It became clear to me, too, that we had fallen into a very peculiar part of the planet. It was good for nothing. Fenced off on the seaward side by cranberry bogs, fenced off on the west by unguessable territory that eventually became America as most people knew it, ending to the north but where, the trees were short and spindling, the soil was essentially sand; I could understand, I suppose, why it was the only stretch of the Eastern Seaboard for hundreds of miles in either direction that showed almost no lights at night—a blotch of darkness upon the lacy webworks that otherwise adorned the edge of this continent. We were come upon a wasteland . . . as was calculated, true, when emergency landing areas were designated, but in fact "emergency landing area" was a sort of joke, wasn't it, intended to somehow give the impression that things were somehow under control somehow even after a crash, but they were not under control, were they? No, they were not under control; nothing was under control.

I came to a field, in the midst of nowhere. I had been moving through scrub pine, precisely—tedious, unsatisfactory stuff, surely useless for any purpose but to break the hearts of people who tried to find some purpose in it. And suddenly, without warning, I came to a clearing.

Thunderstruck, I barely managed to keep myself back in the trees, and peered out at what this might be. And what this might be was an opening in the pines—not so much a field as an opening, unlinked to anything, really, at one margin of which was a small dwelling place that seemed to be cobbled together of whatever came to hand rather than planned, and a truck, very old and badly dented, and motionless forever, I suspected, for the tires were flat, and the windshield was opaque with fractures. It sat at the end of two ruts that disappeared among the trees; only that much road had sufficed to bring it here, to die.

I looked at this, not knowing what to do. I was afraid: to commit, finally, to having intercourse with these people; to having to speak their language; to masquerade as one of them. That was very hard to contemplate. Anything—almost anything at all—and I would delay the moment. And then a dog began to bark, and I retreated back into the woods, and went around the field, and went on; I went on I don't know how long, and came to another place, somewhat like the first but even smaller, in a barely clearing, no truck, no dog, no road at all leading up to it that I could see, and I circled around it and drew closer, eventually: a hovel, without any sign of life—perhaps, I thought, abandoned; a place, I thought, where I might rest and plan my next move, and I pulled aside the rotting blanket that hung over the entrance and ducked quickly inside.

There was only the one room. In the little bit of light that came in the one window, I saw a camp stove, very old and battered, and a chair, and a rickety old chest of drawers, and a cot, bare except for a stained uncovered pillow and a blanket only marginally newer than the one which hung in the doorway. There was no one inside—perhaps had been no one in a long time, I thought, but I suddenly did not care. I think I realized, somehow, that if I were asleep it would not be my fault what happened from then on.

I laid myself down on the cot, and wrapped the blanket around me, and thought that it had been such a long time since I had slept, and so much had happened, so much had changed forever since the last time I had closed my eyes . . . and I slept.

I do not know how long it was before I heard a voice say: "Wake up. Wake up, now." I opened my eyes, hardly knowing where I was, or who, and peered across the tiny room in a growing heart-stopping panic, and saw an old man sitting calmly in the straight chair. He held across his lap a rifle—a single-shot .22, I later learned, with which he hunted small game—and despite this he did not look particularly menacing. He was very old, really, to my far younger eyes. He looked at me and said again, "Wake up, now." And then he laughed, and though technically I could not be sure, because laughter after all might be subtly different here, in fact I was positive, from the first moment I saw him, that he was hopelessly crazy; and I was right . . . the laughter was too free, too delighted by very small things; he was as . . . batty as a bedbug.

Which is not to say that most of the time he was not as sane as anyone. It was, however, to say that his bridges were down, and had been replaced by extravagant structures which were much more daring, if less well able to carry a load, than normal.

His name was Jack English, and he was of an indeterminate age but probably sixty-five or so. He had lived in this spot in the pine barrens for a very long time, as far as I could tell, and I believe at one time he had had a wife, but twenty or twenty-five years ago she had disappeared, and he did not expect to see her again. He laughed again.

He lived, as I said, in the pine barrens, and like most people who lived there he lived on land that was not his own, but did not seem to belong to anyone else, either, and he lived in a house that, basically, he could walk away from in ten minutes, move a mile in any direction, and duplicate in very short order. He had no power or running water, of course; the result was the only constraint on him—that he live near a creek. But he had not actually moved in over twenty-five years.

He told me this, and more, as the morning wore on. I sat on a box, and he sat in a chair.

We conversed. That is, he asked me who I was and what I did; what had brought me to the pine barrens—which was the first I knew of them—and what had brought me to his dwelling place in particular. But when I tried to tell him—that my name was Charlie Mortimer, that I was part of a special Army detachment, that I was lost—he would laugh and call me a liar. Maybe my name was Mortimer, though he doubted it, but that I was part of the U.S. Army he doubted very much, for I carried no military gear, and he doubted if I could be so lost as to be completely separated from the rest of my group; he doubted if I was lost at all. What did I want with him, specifically; why had I come to his dwelling place? And when I tried to tell him I had not come to his dwelling place except by accident, he just laughed and laughed. And finally he said, in his crazy way: "You know what I think, Mr. Mortimer? I think you came down in a flying saucer, and you're trying to fool me. That's what I think. Either that, or you're an escaped prisoner. That's what I think. And you know what, Mr. Mortimer? I don't give a shit, really, as long as you don't pull nothing stupid."

So passed my first morning on Earth. And this is hard to explain, but after a while he showed me how to cook a meal out of a dead squirrel and some flour, and we ate it, from a plate and a cardboard thing like a plate, with a knife for him and a fork for me, and it tasted delicious. Of course, I had not eaten in a long time, but it tasted delicious. And we drank some wine from a glass jug he had, and in due course it was time to go to sleep, the sun going down. And he showed me a corner of the hut where I could bed down, apparently not being at all afraid of me.

And the next day was much the same, and in about a week he went off and came back with a fresh jug and a loaf of bread and some other necessities, though we continued to depend on squirrel and other small creatures for our main dishes, he being very good with the rifle, and the weeks became months and somehow we managed. Sometimes we went days without speaking, once the initial freshet of lies and half-truths was exhausted. I cooked, and did not ask for anything, and this seemed satisfactory to him. That and the occasional night I spent on the bed with him.

And in due course—in a year or two—he let me go to the general store several miles away, on the edge of the barrens, and trade various things, such as cranberries or various things we found in the woods—axes and saws and such, if we were careful, for their owners might notice—for the staples we needed. By then I was wearing a pair of bib overalls, of course. At least, I recall I was . . . there was a certain mistiness to the entire experience . . . and in a few more years, one morning he died. But by then I was acclimated pretty well to life as an Earthman, and in a few weeks I left, with the contents of a buried jar of cash—a hundred and twelve dollars it was, which he had finally shown me the day before he died.

I worked as a dishwasher in a diner for a while, coming out of the barrens, and then I was a day laborer for a while, and then I wrote away for my birth certificate, living in a town called May's Landing. What you do is, you scan the back files of the newspaper until you find an infant that died about the time you want to be born, and you write away for a copy of the birth certificate, and from then on it's you. On the outside.

I think that was the bravest single thing I did. Suppose somebody else had already written for that particular certificate? I got a post office box and everything, and let it lay in the box for a week, and snatched it at last, and left town immediately. Even so, I went clear across the country, by train to Oakland. There I got a job drafting, and living in a room, and thought I would spend the rest of my life in Oakland, which I liked as much as I liked anything. But Eikmo ran into me, or I ran into Eikmo, and I moved to Chicago . . . or, to be precise, Shoreview. And there I ran into Dwuord Arvan, and I knew it was no good, and then eventually I read the paper, and I couldn't help but confront Dwuord, and that was the last straw; it really was.

You must understand that I turned my head and saw that my hand was going to make contact with the third rail, and I could have stopped myself—I thought about the postmortem, but I suddenly realized I would not care.

You understand? It had come down to that. To hell with the whole game. And I reached out my hand deliberately, and died in violet fire.

—Never revealed. A.B.

JACK MULLICA

We came, eventually, to her father's farm—Nick's farm—on the edge of the barrens. It was not much of a farm; the buildings were old, and even the house was swaybacked with age. Nor was it large. But on the other hand, the soil was a little better, there was grass, there were some towering trees which were clearly different from the barren pines. There were outbuildings, including a barn.

The whole layout was not large, but then, Nick Olchuck had long ago given up on the idea of actually making a living from it. There were a few animals—a pair of goats, a hutch full of rabbits, a dog, enough chickens running around to provide eggs for Nick and Margery, and of course cats, which were essentially wild. I knew little of this in detail, as I stood at the edge of the road, supporting a sweaty Margery in the first light of dawn, but one did not need detail to grasp the essentials. The dog, Prince, had come out of the barrel lying on its side beside the barn, where he was chained, and was barking furiously at me.

"Home. Sweet home," Margery said. She called to the dog: "Shut up, Prince. I said, shut up!" and the animal subsided, stood beside his barrel, and regarded me stiffly. Margery turned to me. "All right. You can sleep in the barn. I'll get you some food before I go to work. Now I've got to go inside and explain you to my father."

I looked at her. Up to now, she had been body coolth and bulk and smells, and occasional glimpses, but this was the first time she had stood a little apart from me. Perhaps I had been much the same to her, because she took a minute to look me up and down, too.

She was about my height, and, except for a tendency to too much makeup, not bad-looking. I stood peering at her face for a moment, trying to figure out what was off about it; when I saw her again later, it was less vivid, and her eyes in particular looked much blander, and then I realized it had been makeup. What I did not realize, for years, was that I never actually saw her; she always had some makeup on. But that's beside the point for the time being.

She had a slim, long-legged figure. But it was canted off to one side, and one of her legs was much thinner than the other. She was wearing a dress made out of a chicken feed sack—feed was sold in print sacks, with no company markings, for that express purpose—and she looked out of focus. I found out later that she was only nineteen when I first met her, and one of the purposes of the extreme makeup was to make her look older, but now it was smeared and awry.

"All through?" she said.

"What?"

"Are you all through looking at me?"

I tried a smile. "Yes. You're not bad to look at, you know."

"Bullshit," she said, and turned to go into the house. It was painful to watch her make her way, especially since she knew I was watching her. I went to the barn and lifted the wooden latch, and went inside.

The barn had not been used for anything in particular for a long time. It smelled of something vaguely unpleasant—I learned later it was mildew—but not overwhelmingly so. There were some spots where other odors did overwhelm—cat turds and rat turds—but these were localized, and I avoided them with almost perfect success. There were some feed sacks along one wall, and there were several cats that looked up from sleeping in various nooks as I came in, but that was all. The barn was essentially an empty space enclosed by four walls and a roof. I went over to the feed sacks, and they made a respectable bed. That was my main concern. I was tired enough, God knows. And without further ado I lay down. I thought to myself that life on Earth was a little stranger than it ought by rights to be, and then I was asleep.

I woke up a long time later—late afternoon, it was, by the light that came in through the cracks—and beside me, on the floor of the barn, was an upside-down box that had not been there. I lifted it, and there was a sandwich and a glass of something, red and sweet. Kool-Aid, it turned out. I put the box back down over it and went to the back door, which was jammed shut and hadn't been opened in years. But by tugging on it I got it to open an inch or two and managed to urinate outside. And it struck me funny, for a minute; here was water that had never been on Earth before. But I was not the first, and I went back to the food, which the cats were trying to figure a way into, and smiled, and chased them back, and ate every scrap, including draining the Kool-Aid, which I have not done very often after the first few occasions, for it almost always gives me indigestion. But I was pretty thirsty at the time.

I took stock. There was not much to take. I was in Margery Olchuck's barn after abandoning my crashed flying saucer and the rest of my crew. I had on my issue fatigue uniform, which tended to resemble a coverall jumpsuit, my fatigue shoes, which looked only vaguely Earthlike—until Adidases came along, which was much later—but would pass, and my first-aid kit and my iron rations, which were in two of the patch pockets on my uniform pants.

The iron rations you could keep; we had all eaten one meal of them, in accordance with shipboard drill, and no doubt they would keep body and soul together in a dire emergency. Nobody ever complained. They couldn't—not the ones who actually had to live on the things. The first-aid kit had all sorts of goodies in it, but I did not need any of them. And that was it—oh, I had an identity, Jack Mullica, which was both woefully thin and too well established to abandon. I promised myself that if I were ever to be in a crashing flying saucer again, I would do much better next time.

And that really was it. I considered going into the house to talk to Nick, and felt a mild curiosity that he had not come out to investigate me, but he was too much of a cipher for me to pursue that seriously. I didn't even know his name. So I sat down on the feed sacks, and watched the cats lick the plate and the glass, and scratched one of them behind the ears when it cautiously came over, before it jumped away. And that was it. I wondered what Margery might have in store for me. If not then, then I wondered very often later. I see no reason not to assume that I began that habit in that barn, without knowing it, or at least without knowing what it would cost me, over the years.

It hasn't been that bad.

She came in the evening, carrying more food—a hamburger—and another glass of Kool-Aid. She was wearing jeans and a white T-shirt over a bra. I liked her breasts. She looked tired. She did not look sweet, or girlish. She looked all business. She handed me the food and sat down on the feed bags beside me. "He didn't come in here?" she asked, and I nodded my head, and then remembered and said, "No." She looked at me patiently. "Which is it?" and I said "No" again, and she nodded. "I didn't think so." She shook her head. "He drinks. I drink, too, but he drinks."

"What else does he do?"

"Well, that's about it, really. We're lucky to keep the farm. But he had the mortgage paid off before he started drinking, and my job with the glass company looks pretty solid."

"Glass company?"

"Kimble Glass. In Vineland. I ride the bus. I work in the office; payroll clerk."

Vineland, I presumed, was a town. "What does Kimble Glass do?"

"Medical glassware. We're a division of Owens Corning." I didn't know what that was, but it didn't matter. "When are you planning to move on?"

Move on. I was reluctant to move on. "I don't know. Do you want me to go soon?"

"Eat your supper before it gets cold." Then she looked me right in the eyes and said: "We can't afford to keep you for any length of time."

Well, that had been pretty obvious. I bit into the hamburger. "Is there some kind of work I could do?"

"Where did you say you were going when you bumped into me?"

"I don't believe I said. Nowhere, really."

She nodded. There was infinite knowledge in her eyes. Not judgment; just knowledge. It was hard to face. "You don't have anyplace to go on this continent, do you, Jack Mullica?'' And before I could formulate a reply to that, she said: "It's okay. Some of us who were born here don't have anyplace to go, either." She grinned crookedly. "I don't know. I've got a few people around here who owe me things. Maybe we can find you a job. We'll see."

I had finished my meal. "Look." I had thought this over very carefully. "Look," I said again, "I want you to do me a favor."

"A favor."

"That's right."

"What kind of a favor?"

"I want you to let me try something with your leg."

She stared at me incredulously. Then she burst out laughing. "With my *leg*?" It was not frank and open laughter. After the first instant of genuine shock, it was harsh and mechanical, echoing back from the walls of the barn in sarcasm and anger. She twisted around to face me with her whole body, and the leg was thrust out toward me. "My leg. I've done a lot of favors in my life," she said. "But not with my leg." Then she grinned crookedly. "Or did you mean my good leg?"

I went on doggedly. It was the only way I knew to eventually get through to her at the time, and the time was what I had to work with. So I persisted. "I want to use my first-aid kit on your leg."

"Your what?"

"My first-aid kit." I took it out of its pocket. "I don't know if it'll do any good. But it won't do any harm. I want to try it."

"Oh, yeah. I forgot. Your first-aid kit," she said. "First-aid kit!" She began to laugh again. She reached out and took it. "First-aid kit." She shook her head, then looked more closely. She looked back at me. "I can't read any of the words except Johnson & Johnson."

I shrugged.

She bit her lip momentarily, then looked at me again. "Do you really think it will do any good?" And I heard the faint note of hope underneath everything else she put into the question, which was loaded with carelessness, ninety-nine percent.

"I don't know," I repeated. "It's worth a try."

"Well, what do I have to do?"

I looked down at the floor. "Take your pants off."

She began to laugh again, and I turned on her. "Look, take your pants off or don't; I think I can do you some good, but I may be wrong; if I wanted to copulate with you, I'd at least wait until tomorrow, considering that you haven't even gotten any sleep after your last time; is that clear?"

She had started some reaction, but my choice of words choked it off before it got started. "Copulate with me?" She giggled and put her hand over her mouth, but it did no good; the giggle grew, and turned into a guffaw. She looked at me as if I'd just gotten off the boat, and she couldn't stop laughing. Still laughing, she stood up and opened the belt of her jeans, opened the buttons of the fly front, and pushed the jeans down. She was wearing white cotton panties. She stepped out of the jeans and kicked them aside, and said "Now what?"

still laughing a little, seemingly unaware for a moment how thin and wasted the leg looked in contrast to the good one, and then I saw that in fact she knew exactly how it looked, and she stood there like a young, if tired, queen, and she was utterly in command of the situation. The two of us faced one another in the barn and the relationship cemented itself, right there, nor has it changed to this day, whenever this day is. I pointed to the bags. "Sit down," I said, and she sat, but not as a favor to me—as a favor to herself—and waited.

I opened the kit and took out the tin of muscle stuff. It was intended to help bruises heal faster. It did not work miracles, but it did cut down healing time dramatically. Maybe it would do something for her. "Stretch the leg out," I said, and took two fingertips' worth of the ointment. "Now. Just relax." I wiped the fingers over the outside of the upper thigh, and worked them around. The muscle felt strange, not like a usual muscle at all. But in half a minute the fingertips of my opposite hand, on the inside of her thigh, were slick with the ointment that had come through her leg. I wiped them on the peculiar-feeling muscle there, and worked them, and in a very short while the fingertips of my first hand were slick again. It was working back and forth, a little less emerging out the other side each time, until finally it was gone.

She was looking at me peculiarly. "It's as if I could feel it going all through me," she said. I nodded. "And I taste garlic."

"You taste what?"

"Garlic," she said, a little impatiently.

"Interesting." So now I knew what garlic tasted like. "All right; now we do the rest of the leg." We did the rest of the leg. About a fifth of the ointment had been used. I looked up. "That's all."

She did not move the leg. Her voice was carefully neutral. "Just exactly what do you mean, that's all?"

"That's all I can do, for now. You should feel something—a flush of heat, probably; less impediment to motion; perhaps a little growth in the flesh—within hours. It won't be much, at first. It may never be much. In either case, we'll do some more in twenty-four hours. And maybe something permanent will happen. That's all."

She got off the feed bags, feeling the ground with the toes of her bad leg, twisting it a little, looking down at it. Then she got back into the jeans. "It feels warm," she said.

"That might just be the massage."

"I—don't think so."

"Let it go," I said. "Let it go. It'll start healing or it won't, and what you think of it doesn't matter. What I think of it, too. Just let it go." I stood there, putting the cap back on the ointment, realizing that I had started something from which there was no drawing back. I looked at her, just drawing her belt together, getting ready to button up the fly on her jeans. "All right?"

She had her head down; the wings of her hair fell around her face, and I couldn't see her expression. "All right.'' Then she said: ''Come on in the house; you could use a wash.''

''All right,'' I said.

I met her father. He was sitting in the kitchen, a half-empty glass in front of him, and a bottle beside that. He looked blankly at me as I came into the house. He was in his fifties, I imagined, a square-headed man gone bald on top, with bad teeth and washed-out blue eyes, in an undershirt and work pants. Without changing his expression or raising his voice, he said to his daughter: ''I thought I told you to keep your men out of this house. I said to you, very clearly—''

''He's not one of my men,'' Margery said.

''You expect me to believe that?''

''I'm not a liar.''

He frowned thoughtfully. Than he nodded. ''No. You're not.'' He frowned. ''You're not,'' he repeated. He looked at me. ''That's all right, then. What's his name?''

''My name's Jack Mullica,'' I said. ''I'm pleased to meet you, Mr. Olchuck.'' I stuck out my hand.

He ignored it. ''Are you? Pleased to meet Margery's drunk of a father? I wouldn't be.'' He drank from the glass. ''Go on about whatever business you have here. Don't bother being friendly. I don't really take to it.'' He took another sip. ''On the other hand, I'm not nasty. Count your blessings.'' He looked thoughtful. ''Yes. All in all, I'd say count your blessings.''

"Come on, Jack," Margery said, and tugged at my arm. And I went. What, pray tell, else would I do?

The bathroom was crowded—a sink, the john, and a bathtub with a shower attachment competed for space that left very little bare floor—but it was no worse than the analogous facility on the ship. In fact, it was a little more spacious. In any case, I didn't complain. Earlier that evening, I'd been forced out of the barn long enough to crouch down behind some bushes, and then wipe myself with leaves; that experience makes you appreciate indoor comforts very quickly.

She looked me up and down. "I think some jeans and a shirt of my father's will fit you. And underwear. That'll have to do. All right, I'll leave you now." And she did, with a little flirt of her head that might have meant anything,

But when I was through in the shower—and, oh, it was a *good* shower, once I figured out what it was, and how to work it—there are things you can't learn adequately from television; not even the television of today, and in those days it was much worse—she opened the door a crack and passed through a small heap of clothing which turned out to be as described, with a pair of white cotton socks thrown in. "Pass me your old clothes," she said. "I'll wash them the next time I do laundry."

I did, after taking my iron rations and first-aid kit out of the pockets, and passed my clothes to her. Which left me with the first-aid kit exposed, because it wouldn't fit in any of the jeans pockets. It didn't really matter, I supposed, but I found myself staring at it, and wondering if it was doing her leg any good, and then realizing that it was the only thing, now, that was still mine to control from before the crash. It was an old friend, suddenly. And its content was waning. I stood there with the kit in my hand, looking at the lettering, and the lettering that wasn't lettering, and suddenly I realized I had been down on this planet less than a day, and already I was more Earthman than not. Which was exactly what the people back on my home planet wanted, under these special circumstances. Everything was going well. Everything. I stood there in a bathroom in a marginal farmhouse in borrowed clothes, dependent on a very marginal girl and to some extent on an over-the-edge father; I had no job, no real place to sleep, no money, and everything was going well.

I spent another day in the barn, coming into the house only for a little bit of time at night. The father ignored me. Margery looked at me warily; she seemed, in what few glimpses I had of it, to be setting her leg a little differently, experimentally. But I couldn't be sure, and she seemed to be almost hiding it. After dinner she went back out to the barn with me. "If you want to work on my leg some more, it's all right," she said casually.

"That's right, it *is* twenty-four hours since the last time, isn't it?" I said.

"Yeah." She opened her pants, dropped them, and sat down on the bags. I got out the first-aid kit, and the container of muscle ointment out of the kit, and went over to her. The leg was measurably better. It was less wasted, felt more like a normal leg, and seemed more responsive to stimuli. I did not comment on any of this. I simply applied the ointment, and she simply stared over my shoulder at the wall, her expression completely neutral. The only way you could tell, really, that there was something going on was the fact that she wept, silently and not very hard, but steadily, so that her cheeks were wet when we were finished and she got up and put her pants back on.

"Your hands are warm," she said. "Your whole body's warm. I noticed that from the first. You sick?"

I shook my head, getting it right. I had noticed that she was cold; not much colder than normal, but still . . . "No. It just is that way."

She looked at me for a long time. Then she shrugged and left the barn.

The next day, after work, she came out to the barn, looking at me narrow-eyed, swinging her leg. She walked a lot closer to normal. We neither one of us said anything. It was either working or it wasn't. It appeared to be working. What could you say beyond that, really? Finally she said "Come on" and jerked her head toward something outside the barn. She stood with a hand on the door, and I went over to her.

"What's happening?" I said, and she said, "Get in the car." I looked in the yard, and there was a car there.

—Mullica's recollections, reconstructed

INTERPOLATION, DWUORD ARVAN

It took me a while to get used to the animals—the cats, the dogs, the chickens, and whatnot. They fit their ecological niches in understandable ways, but they weren't the same as the animals we had at home. And it isn't the same to see them on TV and then have them actually rub up against you. It is, as a matter of fact, horrifying at first. Particularly the cats.

But it doesn't take long to acclimate to them; to realize that a cat is profoundly innocent. A chicken has no brain to speak of. A dog seems to have some concept that he is doing something bad, or good, depending on the action. But a cat does everything the same—kills and purrs, plays with a ball of string or a moribund mouse, the same in either case. We have no such thing on my home world; it is unsettling to think too much about cats, and thank your stars they are not larger. But one grows accustomed to them, particularly if one realizes they live pretty much without reference to human beings . . . or us.

What persisted in strangeness was the smells.

That is something for which radio and TV do not prepare you. And it is pervasive; there is nowhere on Earth you can go to escape the smell of Earth.

When we first landed, there was the rich smell of the bog, and then the scent of pines. The one was thick, and clogged the nostrils, and was deceptively familiar, for it was largely the smell of decay. The pines were more difficult: astringent, so that the mucus membranes dried up and tingled, and the throat felt peculiar. But the smell of her, thick with human sweat, cigarette smoke, and liquor, was exotic and oddly titillating, whereas the smell of the farm, with its dog, cat, and chicken feces, its odor of mold and dust in the barn, was hard to take at first.

But it was the cars that really struck me as exotic. They were so different from what we had: different fuel, odd cooling systems, pervasive lubricants. I loved it. I purely loved it. Cars seemed to me to speak more clearly of Earth than any single thing else, and I was going to be of the Earth. I was. It was the only course of action that made sense. Soon enough, I promised myself, no one would be able to tell me from an Earthman . . . at least on the inside.

COURTNEY MASON DOWRIGHT

It is a riverfront home in Maryland. It is not a large home, and the grounds are not extensive. Nevertheless, it is a riverfront home in Maryland.

It is the retirement home of Commander Dowright, who is not yet so frozen by old age that he cannot get up at dawn and, with a gun under his arm and a dog coursing along before him, go for long walks-cum-casual-shootings. But Commander Dowright does not actually do that very often. Most of the time, he sits out on his back porch and broods, bitterly. When I found him, he was glad to talk. He raised the tape recorder to his lips and said:

My name is Courtney Mason Dowright, and I was, at the time of my assignment to determine exactly what was going on at NAS Atlantic City, a commander in the United States Navy. I am now retired, of course.

There were several peculiarities about the call to Philadelphia Naval District Headquarters. Minor in themselves, they led to the inevitable conclusion that, once again, Fred Andrews was doing nothing to disprove the grading that had made him graduate almost dead last in his year at the Academy. (Frederick Mayhew Andrews was a captain in the U.S. Navy at the time, and commanding officer of NAS Atlantic City, not a plum job. He was scheduled to retire later that year, still a captain, and would have been retired earlier if the opening at Atlantic City had not needed a man for a short while, until his successor had completed certain courses. For that matter, it is problematical that he would have been a captain in the first place if so many other better men hadn't been killed or invalided out in the war.)

But a three A.M. telephone call from a commanding officer to a district headquarters—any commanding officer, any district headquarters—leaves the district headquarters with few options. So I in turn was knocked out of bed and told that something worth my time was going on down at NAS Atlantic City, though no one at Philadelphia was sure what. That was the first thing I was to find out for sure. And in due course after that I was helicoptered down to NAS Atlantic City, where in due course after *that* I learned that a congressman had somehow gotten involved.

Upon learning that he was a Navy veteran, I at first took this for an encouraging sign. But I am getting ahead of myself.

Upon landing, I was taken to Fred Andrews. In his

office, alone with him, I learned that the base might have a visitor from another planet. It might almost equally well have a convincing madman, or some third possibility, but whoever or whatever he was, he was wearing badges that could not be read, and he had brought with him a similarly attired corpse who was not the world's prettiest sight.

I sat back and looked at Captain Andrews for a while, making up my mind tentatively. This was after the first big rash of reported flying saucer sightings—we had not yet learned to call them UFOs—in 1947 and '48, including quite a few by Navy personnel. And I was as aware as he that there were persistent rumors the Navy, or somebody, actually had some corpses, possibly even some live crewmen. But nothing solid; only reports of rumors, and I, of course, no more actually knowledge-able than anyone else in the Navy as far as I knew.

Well, that was what you would expect. If some base somewhere had solid evidence, that base was now but-toned up pretty good. In fact, that base was leading two lives: one, that nothing had ever happened there, and two, that for the few personnel that knew different, life was very complicated indeed.

Because anybody who thought the United States was going to make off-world visitors—we had not yet learned to call them extraterrestrials—public, or even private, didn't have his head screwed on right. And the same for every other government on Earth.

Why? Because if it was a small government, it knew perfectly well the big governments would take an immediate, intense, and personal interest, which could not possibly be good for the small government. And if it was a big government, then it knew it was at the top of the technological heap on Earth, the visitors were bound to be advanced beyond that, so, ipso facto, the big government could do nothing real to protect its citizens, or say it was protecting them, from whatever. And that inevitably leads to anarchy, which is the thing governments like least of all.

So, inasmuch as the visitors, if any, had somehow chosen not to announce themselves to Earthpeople so far, the best course was to hunker down and pray they would turn out to be an illusion, would at the very least continue to play coy, or we would, in the fullness of time, surpass them technologically. I suppose. Frankly, the last possibility struck me as unlikely in the extreme, since presumably the visitors weren't obligingly standing still developmentally, either. On the first two choices, I had at that time an opinion divided exactly fifty-fifty.

But be that as it may, the immediate question was, what was Captain Andrews going to do? So I quickly pointed out that Captain Andrews was only an inch or two away from safe retirement, and Captain Andrews huffed and grunted that of course he knew that and he was of course turning the entire matter over to me as the representative of the Philadelphia Naval District and I said no other thought had crossed my mind for even a moment, and that was that. Then I said let's go look at the corpse and then let me interview this man you've got, and that was when I learned about the congressman.

The congressman was young, junior in rank, and many miles from his home district. But he was indefatigable, in the sense that he was rapidly developing a reputation for going anywhere and doing anything that would inch him up the ladder, and heavyweights in the system had cautiously marked him as a comer.

He was at the base on a visit with some servicemen from his home state, having brought one of them a medal for heroism in a fire, said heroism having been performed while the serviceman in question was home on liberty. An innocuous errand having nothing to do with the congressman's being a junior member of the House Armed Services Committee, and I looked at Captain Andrews with almost open incredulity when I heard that. But then I remembered that the congressman was ex-Navy, and I almost relaxed for a moment. After all, too, this was not the first congressman to think up some excuse for enjoying the free perks of a service installation instead of paying for a hotel room.

So I let that one go by. And apparently that *was* the congressman's motive—or else whatever his motive actually was, it was derailed in favor of the one he had been presented with this morning. Because I never heard of any other trouble at the base as a result of the congressman's visit. Not that—ah, hell with it; I never heard of any other trouble, there is no reason to think there ever was any other trouble brewing, and what I'm saying is that life's too short for some people to keep up with all the possibilities the congressman presented over the years. But now I'm getting beyond myself, and certainly beyond the point you're interested in, right?

So. We went down to where the corpse was, in among the gray narrow corridors, the captain and I, and found him in the morgue. We dismissed the morgue attendant, and I pulled out the drawer.

I did not learn much. He did not look any different from a man to me, he was dressed in coveralls which were slightly different from those one normally saw, but not outlandishly so, and they were marked with badges I could not read and did not look like they were in any language I had ever seen—and I have seen quite a few, as have most people who have served in the Navy for any length of time. But there were several explanations for my not recognizing the language, and most of them did not require that the lettering be part of a coherent system in use on some other world.

The man *had* died hard; the middle of his body was not a pretty sight. There remained enough, however, to assure us he was a man. Frankly, it was difficult to believe in him being off-world after seeing his genitals; blackened and burned, of a good size, rather they cried out pitifully that a man like ourselves lay there, in worse case than we fervently prayed we would ever be. I turned away. "That's enough," I said. "I'll come back for him later," and we left.

We moved up one flight to where the prisoner was. And on the way we were joined by the congressman.

It was my first meeting with him, and I was immediately struck by his intensity, and by the fact that it was not in particular directed at me. Rather, he seemed to have an invisible opponent in play, and I—and everyone else—was not as important. Other than that, he was pleasant and polite. I got the distinct feeling that he would always be pleasant and polite as long as he did not feel compelled to study you closely. I wondered what I could do to keep him that way.

Fat chance.

Anyway, there we were, in the corridor outside the prisoner's room, with an armed guard at the door, and the congressman seemed to have materialized out of thin air, although actually he had simply stepped out of an adjacent room. How he knew it was us, and not more casual traffic, was easy—he had kept one eye to the crack in the slightly open door. But until you realized that, there was something just a bit disconcerting about it.

"You're going to speak to him now?" the congressman asked, and when I allowed that yes, indeed, that was what I was there for, he nodded. "Of course. Well, you'll speak to me afterward. Correct?"

Well, not correct, exactly. There was no reason in the world for me to speak to him—or the commanding officer, for that matter—afterward. My report was technically for the admiral commanding the naval district.

But I could see now that this would lead to a confrontation with the congressman, and one thing the admiral did not want was a confrontation with any congressman. And certainly not this one, on brief acquaintance. The fact was that the Navy was, as usual in peacetime, fighting to keep every friend it had in the House and Senate. So I smiled frankly and openly, and said "Of course, sir," and he did his best to smile openly and frankly, too. "Very good," he said, and I went in to the Martian or whatever he was with a definite feeling of unease.

He was behind his table and yawning into his hand when I came in, and gesturing in embarrassment with his other arm as his jaws gaped wider and wider and his eyes screwed themselves shut. "Sorry," he said a moment later, collecting himself. "It's been a while since I slept. And your name is . . . ?"

"Court Dowright. And yours is what?"

He grinned. "Well, so far I've been claiming it's Ditlo Ravashan, and I say I am a member of a civilization that takes in more than just your Sun."

"Ah." I pulled out a chair and sat down opposite him. "And is this true?"

"Which? That I claim it, or that my claim is true, or both?"

I looked at him. If we were going to play that sort of verbal game, we could be here a long time. On the other hand, the longer we played it, the likelier it was that the man was, simply, a man. Frankly, looking at him, I found it quite difficult to believe he had come out of a flying saucer. "Both," I said.

"Well," he said with a faint twinkle in his eye, "I have claimed it. And it might be true."

That eye—those eyes—were a peculiar shade of brown. I wondered if he might not have on a pair of tinted contact lenses, which were just coming into limited use at the time.

"Are you crazy?" I asked.

He threw back his head and laughed. "Well, if I am—and I might be—I'm not really the right person to ask, am I?"

"Where is your ship?"

"If there is one, it's lost in the bogs." He waved as if he knew which way the room faced; in actual fact, he waved at the North Atlantic. "Somewhere out in the bogs. We would have hidden it, and we would have done a good job."

"We?"

"Oh, the other man and I."

"The other man was moribund."

"But he would have been alive at the time."

"Would have been."

He laughed again. "Yes. Would have been."

"You're really not saying anything, are you?"

"Well, yes and no."

I was not prepared to take any more of that. The man had an accent, and he had somewhat peculiar eyes, but the rest of him as far as I could tell was as normal as normal could be. We could have spent a year in that room together, and if he wanted to keep playing verbal games, and if I kept to playing verbal games, we would be no further along at the end of that year than we were right that minute. I pushed back my chair. "This really isn't very satisfactory. I'll be back," I said, and left. The man was smiling at me as I went.

They had taken away his first-aid kit; the armed guard outside his door had it. I examined it. It had several things in it which were obviously machine-produced, and the lettering was (A) machine-produced and (B) unreadable except for the Johnson & Johnson. But that, too, could easily have been produced on Earth. Nothing said the gadgets actually had to do anything. All it told me, really, was that someone had gone to a great deal of trouble and expense to create the kit.

But that, too, depended on the scale of size. For a national government, for instance, or even one considerably down the ladder from that, it would have been nothing. Perhaps more important, even for one man with hidden motives, if it had to be consistent with his story, it could certainly be done. In other words, the first-aid kit, for me in my situation, answered no questions definitively; rather, it perhaps raised a few additional ones. Or perhaps not.

I gave it back to the guard, a little annoyed that I had ever looked at it at all.

"What do you think?" the congressman said to me.

We were sitting in the adjacent room, just the two of us, not much different from the room with the man in it—except that I was facing the door, I suddenly realized, and the congressman was between me and it—and the congressman was pretending it was just a casual question. Well, I'd tell him the truth. Anything else was too dangerous. "I don't know," I said. "I know less, I suppose, than I did before I got here."

"You suppose. Yes. It all has a tendency to raise more questions than it answers, doesn't it?" The congressman suddenly turned a smile on me, and I felt peculiar. Later, I finally decided it was because it was a perfectly friendly smile, and it chilled me to the bone.

"You know what I think? I think you will give him to me." The congressman was quite serious.

"What?"

"Look at it from all sides," the congressman said reasonably. "This isn't really a Navy matter. It would be different if the Navy knew more, perhaps. But all that happened was that the man turned up at your main gate in the middle of the night. He said only the minimum to the enlisted personnel, he said only enough more to the officers to work his way swiftly up the chain of command, and he still isn't saying much, is he?"

"Not now, no."

The congressman waved his arm—in much the same way that the man had. "That's as may be. The fact is, he isn't talking."

"Sir, I—"

"The chances are excellent he's a man with a hidden agenda. Period. The chances that he's actually the captain of a flying saucer are—"

"That's not the point! He's—"

The congressman steepled his fingertips and looked at me. "That is the point, Commander. That's very much the point. The man might be any number of things, of which the least likely is that he's the captain of a flying saucer. Furthermore, he's begun backing away from that claim. I think you should go back to Philadelphia, report to your admiral that the man was unbalanced—which he almost certainly is, wouldn't you say?—and let it go at that. I'm sure the Navy has a great many other things on its mind. For instance, the next appropriations bill."

"Sir, I don't think that's quite the truth."

"Oh?" The congressman looked down at his hands. "Do you know what the truth is? Suppose I told you that in fact Congress has a subcommittee devoted to investigating flying saucer claims, and that the duty of every member of Congress is to bring in any scrap of evidence he happens to come across?"

"Is that true, sir?"

The congressman spread his arms. "You see?"

I shook my head. I felt I was getting deeper and deeper into a morass. "I don't know—"

The congressman looked at me as if I were not too bright a child but he was choosing not to point that out to me. "Commander," he said, "there are only two basic explanations for the man. One, he is what he at one time was saying that he was. In which case, do you suppose the Navy is superior to the national legislature in dealing with it? Or the man is a hoax, in which case the Navy wants to be rid of him as soon as possible. Now, isn't that a fair summary of the situation?"

"Congressman, I—"

Now the congressman looked closely at me, and I knew I had crossed a line I devoutly wished to get back to the safe side of as soon as possible. "Commander," he said softly, "do you perhaps have a hidden allegiance which makes you so stubborn?"

This was the late 1940s, remember. "A hidden allegiance" meant the Soviet Union, and there was no surer way to spend the rest of one's life essentially as a hunted animal than to become identified with that. You think it's bad now; that was the day of Joe McCarthy. I straightened up as though jolted with an electric current, and said "No, sir!" as brightly and innocently as I could manage. And on that question, I made it my business to manage every volt that I could, plus some extra I usually didn't use.

"Then what's the problem, Commander?" The congressman was looking at me hard.

"Sir, I have a responsibility to my mission—"

"And how would you be failing to meet it?"

"Sir, I came down here—"

The congressman shook his head in mild exasperation. "And you will go back up, and make your report. The base commander certainly won't contradict it. A couple of enlisted men will be transfered, but in fact they don't know—nobody knows—what actually transpired here. The junior officers he talked to don't know for sure. The base commander doesn't actually know for sure. And *you* don't know, do you? Do you, Commander?''

He was right. I didn't know. I suspected. And what I suspected was that the man was playing some game far beyond me; that he hadn't come down in a flying saucer, which was ridiculous, but that he was playing some elaborate game. Which, in fact, was more properly in the hands of the national legislature than it was in the Navy's.

''And what do I do with the corpse?'' I asked.

''Why, you give it to the man. He'll know what needs to be done with it. Give it to the man, packed in dry ice. Give us the use of an ambulance for a few hours, and it'll then be as if it had never been. The water will have closed seamlessly.''

And that is how it was. The driver returned with the ambulance from National Airport in Washington, the man and the congressman and the corpse having gotten out there and from there could have gone anywhere, and it was not until I was in the helicopter going back to Philadelphia that it gradually dawned on me my Navy career was irretrievable blighted. Because the admiral commanding the Philadelphia District could not know for certain that I was telling him the whole truth, but on the other hand he did not dare put me on trial to determine that fact. So he made sure I never advanced beyond commander, because a man who might know as much as I did could not be trusted with higher command. Oh, I might in fact be under the protection of persons in the Navy higher than he, but if they moved to intervene on my behalf, they would show their hand. So they would not move to intervene on my behalf.

And so forth. You see what I'm saying? It was impossible for *anyone* to deal with Ravashan—or whatever his name was—and remain untainted. And it was impossible to get at the truth of the man. And that was that. The base commander died a long time ago, of old age, and the junior officers have many other things to think about, and the enlisted men are scattered, and none of us is getting any younger.

For that matter, you don't know that what I've told you is the truth, the whole truth, and nothing but the truth, do you? It is, but you don't *know* that, do you?

And Commander Dowright smiles bitterly.

—Statement taken in 1973. A.B.

FOOTNOTE

Commander Dowright was quite correct. Whereas up to then his fitness reports had been outstanding, they show a peculiar shift after his visit to NAS Atlantic City. It is not something one can put his finger on legally; the words of praise are still there. But when you put them all together, they give a sense that they add up to "a loyal and thoughtful officer, considering what he is." It is not necessary, of course, for the reports ever to say exactly what he is.

—A.B.

CARS

It was a '39 Chevrolet, I found out later, four-door, with the six-cylinder inline nailhead engine—stick shift, of course—a car there, with a man behind the wheel, watching me as I walked up.

"It's all right," Margery said to me. "He's a friend." That seemed hardly likely, since he didn't even know me. What she meant was, she was willing to vouch for him. The other thing was that she had uttered an undoubted cliché; I had heard it issue from the mouths of actor after actor, and if I had heard it so often, how many additional times must it have been uttered? But then I realized something else. Margery was no dummy, but she was a rustic, and I was going to get just so much a range of utterances out of her. Well, so be it. There are worse things to be than a rustic.

"All right." I nodded; that was twice I'd gotten nodding right. As for whether she was trustworthy enough to vouch for anyone, that was an order of question that was beyond me to judge. "Okay," I said. "And?"

"He wants to talk to you about a job."

"Really?" He was in his middle twenties, I found out, a spare, blue-jawed man with black hair that hung over his forehead in oily spikes. He was wearing farm clothes—a blue chambray shirt and bib overalls—and a cigarette dangled out of a small, thin-lipped mouth. I went around to the driver's window. "Hello," I said, watching him carefully. "I'm Jack—"

"Mullica," he said. His mouth twisted into a mirthless grin. "My name's Roland Lapointe. Get in." He gestured toward the passenger seat in front and waited for me, his eyes appraising me while I made up my mind. I finally walked around to the other side of the car and got in. Margery got into the backseat, and Lapointe drove out of the farmyard. The engine ticked over flawlessly; Lapointe, or somebody, had taken very good care of it during the war.

"That's the ticket," Lapointe was saying. "I like my people to do what they're told."

I glanced at him. "Your people."

"When you work for me, you're my people."

"And what makes you think I'll work for you?"

"Haven't got much choice. Can't expect Margery to keep feeding you for free. Can't expect to live in the barn forever—it's all right now, but winter does come."

"I could get another job."

"Not if I say no. Nobody'll give you a job if I say not to. Now, suppose you sit and think about that until we get to where we're going." His voice was flat; he might have been giving the time of day.

I glanced at him again. As far as I could tell, he also hadn't changed expression once while speaking. I got the definite impression Lapointe was a genuinely tough man. Maybe not the brightest. But his outstanding quality would always be his toughness; it would carry him far. Doubtless, it had carried him far already. The important thing was, he was tougher than I.

Well, come to that, Margery was tougher than I. The jury was out on Margery's father, but the likelihood was that he was at least as tough as I. So as far as I knew, every single inhabitant of Earth was tougher than I. It made a fellow proud to be a soldier.

We drove along. Lapointe turned several corners, and we left unpaved surface and pulled onto a main road, though it was still only two lanes of asphalt. We passed several farms. Then we came to a corner. We pulled up outside a structure I recognized as a garage.

There were two things out front that were gas pumps, obviously, and then there were actually a couple of buildings—a small one in front and a much bigger one about twenty-five yards back from both roads, set behind the small building and separated from it by a driveway. The small building had a window with oil jars in it, and in front of the building were several oil drums.

I studied it with some intensity. We don't depend anywhere near as much on individual transport as Earthpeople do, though there was a time when we did. Now our cars and trucks run on a modification of a spaceship engine. The roaring, stinking, polluting Earth car was utterly foreign to me. And utterly intriguing. The idea of getting into your own vehicle and roaring off at speeds of about a hundred miles per hour and going on for miles—far more miles than apparently made sense in a culture with plentiful trains, planes, and buses— and having a garage on practically every street corner in most parts of the nation . . . well, it was grotesque. And it was quaint. And it was, in its own way, glorious.

We forget, now; so much is different. But that was the time when America was the undoubted leader in the world, and gasoline was twenty-five cents a gallon, and cars—new cars—cost a thousand dollars, and the United States was about to buy a highway system that would cover the country from one end to the other, *replacing* a highway system that was the envy of all other nations. I understood, even then, that without question the best way to understand these people was to understand their infatuation with cars. And apparently I was going to get my chance.

"All right," Lapointe said. "What I'll want you to do is tend the garage. Pump gas, fill tires, hand out road maps, tell people the john is out of order. You won't be a mechanic. I'll take care of that. You'll sleep inside at night, you'll get three meals a day, and a dollar a day. Sundays we're closed."

"You're offering me that job."

"Yes."

"I don't know how to drive."

Lapointe turned in his seat and looked back at Margery.

"So teach him," she said. "How hard can it be?"

Lapointe looked at me. "Um."

Lapointe had gone into the other building. Margery and I were alone. "Listen," Margery said to me, "he's all right. He's hard. But he's all right." And she had brought my kit; the coveralls, and the kit. She sat on the corner of the battered desk in the garage, with her pants down around her ankles, while I worked on her. There was something a little bit evasive about her all of a sudden, and that had to be Lapointe, but she flexed and moved the leg almost normally, and she spoke to me in a tone that was much gentler than the one she used to use.

"You keep your nose clean, and you'll be all right," she was saying. "Don't jump to any hasty conclusions. And I'll be around. You got any questions, you ask me first. Got that?"

I cocked my head. "What's wrong?" I said.

"Nothing's wrong unless you screw up. And you won't screw up all the way; you've got sense, even if it isn't horse sense."

"Look, Margery—"

"I owe you more than you can imagine," she said, sliding off the desk and pulling up her pants. "You can't dream how much what you're doing to my leg means to me. But that's not the only thing in the world.

Anyway, I got you the best job you could possibly get. You'll learn to drive, you'll get a Social Security card, pretty soon you'll blend right in with us Americans.''

"What do you mean?" I asked with a sinking feeling.

"Jack," she said, looking at the floor, "you wouldn't fool a four-year-old right now. There's only one place you could have come from, and that's a Russian ship. Probably a submarine. All right? Get this through your head—*we* don't care. You obviously aren't here to commit sabotage. Chances are you're glad to get away. I know I would be—it doesn't sound like a decent way for the ordinary guy to live, communism. All right; fine. We'll help you. And if some of the things we ask in return aren't exactly legal, well, what's legal?"

It was my turn to look down at the floor. "I see."

"So you keep your nose clean, and we'll gradually make an American out of you."

"Yes."

"And I really do thank you for my leg. I didn't know you people could do that. I'm grateful."

"Yes, well."

"And if you want to bed me, that's all right, too." Both of us were looking at the floor.

Things were going too fast for me. "I—what about Lapointe?"

"Lapointe is my brother. Half-brother. We've got the same mother. Came out of the barrens, settled with old man Lapointe first, when he died she moved in with my old man. One day Pop woke up and she was gone.

Found out she hitched a ride on the highway. Last anybody here has seen of her.''

"My God."

Margery shrugged. "It was a long time ago, now. She wasn't the first funny thing that came out of the barrens." She looked at me. "Wasn't the last. Though I will say, it wasn't usual for somebody from the barrens to name themselves for the Mullica River.''

Things at Lapointe's Garage settled into a routine very quickly.

Roland did teach me how to drive, by the simplest method, which was to sit me behind the wheel in the middle of a large open field, point out the accelerator, brake, and clutch and the functions of each, and then stand back and let me stall out a few times, swing around wildly a few times, damned near run into a tree a few times even if this meant wandering far afield, and fairly soon learn to coordinate everything. I did not, of course, tell him that I knew how to drive our ground cars. He, on the other hand, did not tell me that I was a good driver, which I very soon was.

The name of the town, if it can be called a town, was Phyllis. The name of the next town was Wertenbaker. The name of the town three miles down a side road, fronting a lake, was Serena Manor. At some early point in our relationship, Margery explained this to me. Daniel Wertenbaker had named Phyllis for his daughter, and Serena Manor for his wife. There was no particular reason for the towns in the first place; of the combined population of about three hundred, two hundred fifty were engaged in raising chickens, one of the few crops that would grow profitably on the soil. The narrow spaces in the woods that the three towns represented were crammed with two-and three-story chicken coops, housing well over a million chickens, and they smelled like it. At night you could hear the chickens snoring. During the day you could hear them eating, and pecking weaker chickens to death.

Margery came to see me every day after work, and I used up all of my muscle balm. By the time I did that, she was walking normally, and it would have taken a very sharp eye to detect the difference between her legs; in effect, there was none.

She had to account for it somehow. At first, it had been a sort of miracle, but one that could fail. The leg could go back to what it had been. The whole thing might have been some kind of illusion born of hope. But now it wasn't failing, and if she didn't find some way to account for it, there were too many questions to ask about me. And she saw me every day, and I worked in a garage. What could be mysterious about me?

"It's the Sister Kenny treatment, isn't it?" she said, referring to a long, hard course of hot towels and massage that only worked sometimes, and only if it was started the minute the paralysis set in. "Some variation on the Sister Kenny treatment."

"Yes," I said. "A variation on it," as if I really knew what I was talking about. And she brightened up.

"That explains it,"

"Absolutely." As long as you didn't question it. And what do you suppose the chances were of her ever questioning it once she had hit upon Sister Kenny in the first place? She flirted the leg back and forth, feeling the power and the weight-carrying capacity of it. If she spoke of it skeptically, ever, might not the charm be broken? She licked her lips and nodded.

"Yes," she said very softly. The offer to bed her was still good, I knew. I wanted to, but somehow I felt that it was too soon, and that Lapointe would hear us, and that—in truth, I wanted to, very much, but the thought of interspecies . . . well, I would get to it, but it would take some getting used to—I was scared. I was scared green. I'd had one or two women, not many, and I was afraid of all the usual things, plus giving myself away. I had no idea what the sexual appendage of an Earth male looked like. Whereas Margery knew very well. It would take special circumstances, and they had not yet occurred. And so we each had a secret thing between us.

I know it puzzled Margery that I did not take her up on the offer. But she was too polite to come out and ask me directly. I also presumed that the creation of a good leg meant, among other things, a change in her sex life . . . more discrimination, certainly; perhaps even complete abstinence until she could fully assimilate the change, and fully assimilate the idea that she could be choosier than in the past.

I gradually learned Lapointe's real business. Once or

twice a month a tow truck dragging a car would pull up to the other building in the middle of the night, and once or twice a month a car would emerge from the building, a different color and usually with different accessories than when it went in at the end of a hook. The car would be driven away by Christie, Roland's right-hand man, and the following day, late, Christie would come back on the bus.

Christie was about five feet three inches tall, and I presume the lack of height weighed on him; he was muscular, young, and handsome, but didn't have a sense of humor at all. He kept to himself and handed Roland his tools.

In due course—it was the spring—Christie did not come back. Well, it was a weak point in Roland's system; there was nothing to compel Christie to come back, if he chose instead to keep the car, or the money from the car, and go and do something else thereafter. There was really little likelihood Roland would spare the time and trouble to find him. And if he found him, the money would likely already be spent.

Roland went around in a black rage. Finally I said to him: "Roland."

"What?"

"Roland, what if I were to deliver the cars?"

Roland gripped me by the upper arm in a hold that bruised flesh. "What the hell do you know about it?"

The hold was not comfortable. But I pretended not to mind it. "I've got eyes. I know Christie takes the cars somewhere. I know he didn't come back. If the authorities had him, they would have been here by now. The other possibility is he's in cahoots with whoever receives the cars, but that makes no sense because that man would cut off his source of supply if he offended you. So Christie did this on his own. All right—from now on, I'll be Christie. The difference is, I'll always come back.''

"Will you?" Roland frowned. "Why?"

"Because Margery's here," I said, and it was the truth. Somehow, without really meaning to, I had built up too many ties to cut.

Roland grinned mirthlessly. "Yes. Little Sis Margery. Little Margery that's no longer crippled. I wonder how much I believe in Sister Kenny. I wonder, if it's that easy, why don't more people use it." His eyes were very sharp on my face for a minute. Then he shrugged. "All right," he said, and it was a moment before I realized he had okayed the deal. "All right," he said again. "You gonna stick with the Mullica name?"

"It's my name," I declared, because, after all, what else could I do?

"Right," he said.

"What difference does it make?" I asked a little testily.

"Gonna show up on your driver's license, that's why," he said, and walked away to use the phone.

And that is how I got a birth certificate, and then a Social Security card, and a driver's license in the name of Jack Mullica: on the strength of one phone call from

Roland Lapointe to someone who could forge the basic document.

To this day, nobody ever checks back to the original issuing authority for the validity of the birth certificate. If you present the purported certificate in another state, the odds are very low of the particular clerk's even knowing what a genuine certificate should look like. For that matter, states themselves change the appearance of their birth certificates from time to time. I presume the appearance of my certificate is actually genuine for its time frame. I don't actually *know*—no one has ever questioned it, and I have never seen another one.

I took it, when I got it, to the Social Security office in Mays Landing, and to the driver's license station in Atlantic City, and in about as much time as it takes to tell, I was a valid citizen of the United States of America. Eventually I got a fake draft card, and that was a bit of a risk, but not as much of a risk as a physical examination would have been. I had to explain to Roland that I was a bit old to just take the exam in the regular way. He grumbled, but he saw the sense of it. In any event, no one has ever asked to see it. I marvel at such a country—I don't complain.

—Reconstruction. A.B.

FOOTNOTE

A check of records bears out that Mullica obtained them as just outlined. The documents all either are forgeries or emanate from forgeries. The birth certificate is in fact rather crude, containing inks not available at the time of the supposed birth, and being countersigned by the wrong names. But no one subjects the ink and paper to analyses, and who knows what the right names are?

The draft card is rather good. It would have to be, since it was required by law to be carried on the person, and was subject to inspection at any time. But Mullica was never asked for it, apparently. From time to time he would have to record the pertinent data on work applications and the like, but in that case the persons asking for the data did not ask to see the draft card. Nor, given the nature of the times, did anyone ever check the data; they simply filed it together with the rest of his employment data.

Until I began the research for this book, I had no idea how porous the systems of identification really are in this country. No wonder Americans are forever getting into trouble on visits overseas, where there are much stricter controls no child of Uncle Sam will tolerate well.

—A.B.

STATEMENT, DITLO RAVASHAN

The Navy truck let off Yankee at one end of National. Then it drove to the other end, and the driver helped me with the crate with Joro and the dry ice in it. There were no benches; I sat on the crate and watched the truck go around a turn and disappear from this account. It was a little chilly. The crate fumed CO_2 gas through its narrow bottom slots. Once a man going by eyed the crate thoughtfully. "Lobsters," I said, and the man nodded and went on his way, without saying, "On dry ice?"

I watched the women. I had plans. Most of the women were dogs, but every once in a while a good-looking one went by, her physical attributes evident even in her topcoat. I pictured them at my feet, beside themselves, crying out like the animals they were, and this helped pass the time.

After about an hour, a plain station wagon came

cruising down the ramp and stopped in front of me. Henshaw—he introduced himself—was driving it: an ugly, appealing black man, well dressed, in his early thirties, who did not waste my time with small talk. He looked me in the face, and when he shook my hand, he looked at my wrist. Something behind his eyes nodded to itself. But he didn't say anything. He took his end of the crate, we wrestled it aboard, and were on our way.

We crossed the river and stopped at a motel. "You've got a reservation," Henshaw said. He told me the name. "It's already paid for. All you have to do is get your key. Tomorrow, or the next day at the latest, we'll have an apartment for you. And some clothes. Meanwhile, I strongly suggest you get some sleep. And order your food in from room service." He reached behind him and handed me a brown paper shopping bag. "Razor, toothbrush, and so forth." He looked at my jaw again. What he said was "Good luck," and he and Joro's corpse drove away. I went into the motel, and commenced my life as an American.

I had been right, when I carefully misused the engines on my craft—it would be a very good life for me here. Much better than it would have been on my home world. I had seen the retired captains on my home world; they did not look happy. They looked as though they had lost something, out in the stars. As indeed they had; they had grown old, out among the stars, and had had to come home, finally, and gradually dry up, and blow away.

It was a long run on Earth for me, and I enjoyed it immensely. We got me an apartment in Georgetown, and I enjoyed its amenities. I did not go out of town and leave it very often; I did not need to, and I did not want to. Why take chances?

We also acquired a very nice house in Georgetown, quite nearby, and that is where the National Register of Pathological Anomalies settled in after we got government funding. I ran it with a phone at first, and then computers, and I never set foot in the NRPA offices. Why should I? The NRPA occasionally sent a message to its "parent organization," and I would answer it, and that was that—the NRPA was staffed by conscientious civil servants, and they ran the routine daily in an exemplary manner. They even did a lot of good for pathology departments across the nation; well worth the taxpayer's dollar. And meanwhile I took in the recreational delights of Earth.

Not to put too fine a face on it, I had no qualms about using prostitutes, often black and in pairs, which I did with imagination and gusto. A permanent attachment seemed much too risky to me. It meant I would never have a wife, but that hardly mattered; I was not going to have children in any event, and I counted that, as a matter of fact, among my advantages. For one thing, I did not have to go through the stultifying mechanics of contraception.

Prostitutes are cheaper, and one does not have to

entertain them with small talk. I met them in hotels all over town for years, and many a memorable time we had. It really is amazing what you can get the animals to do if you make the rewards big enough for them. And I had plenty of reward to distribute.

I proceeded to make Yankee very rich, you see, a procedure he took to very well. I began by having him manufacture shoes like mine, through a dummy corporation, and though there were imitators very soon, that was to be expected—and Yankee owned some of the imitators, too. Then there was the deceptively simple aerosol valve, which alone would have sufficed to make him a multimillionaire if he hadn't had to split it with the front man. And the new way to make a milk carton, the razor that was a continuous strip of razor-sharp steel in a compact head, and so on.

Several things were to be remarked on about all this. For one thing, I got my split, of course, and not even I could spend it as fast as it came in. For another, Yankee, no matter how wealthy he became, did not lose his primary drive, which was not for power, which he soon had to a nearly incalculable point, and not so much for a public awareness of his actual power, which awareness wavered with his fortunes and was never very accurate. Rather, it was for public awareness that he commanded mysterious and fundamentally, deliberately unknowable power. *That* was more important to him than any other single thing on Earth, by far. It created a peculiar aura around him. Nobody liked him. Nobody loved him—and this bothered him. But everyone kowtowed to him, and that, it seems, was what he held most precious.

And for a third, it would take an inspection team from my home world about thirty seconds to determine that this was too much to be a coincidence; someone was feeding Earth this information. So there was some risk, but it was on the order of requiring Earth to be the subject of an inspection, and then it required the inspection team to find me. I thought I had made that rather difficult for them. But in any case you will notice that none of the information was strategic or tactical.

Well, actually, when I gave him the secret of the transistor, it was a close call. But in fact several laboratories on Earth were about to discover it for themselves, and all we did was jump the gun by, literally, months. And I did not so much give him the secret of the transistor—which I did not fully know—as alert him to the possibility. He was the one who found the work at Bell Labs and elsewhere much advanced. So that was all right. And of course the patents were quickly superseded, and improvements on the original design came thick and fast and were patented by others. But I'm sure you will agree that with a device as fundamental as the transistor, you can spill ninety-nine parts in a hundred, and still realize quite a nice profit. As we certainly did.

As I say, it was a generously nice run. For a time, Yankee restlessly wanted more information about my home civilization, and data such as the engineering behind the spaceship engine drive. But the fact is I couldn't have given him the latter if I had wanted to—

what would a pilot have to know about engineering, as distinguished from inconspicuous unbalanced use of the engines?—and the former, he quickly realized, could have been made up or couldn't have been made up, and how was he to know? So our arrangement was not quite what he had expected, but it did make him filthy rich, and he quickly accommodated to it.

And he found ways to use it, nevertheless. I'm sure he told very selected people about me, and what I represented. What else accounts for his rise in American politics? Other people were easily on the same side as he on the Communist question, and other people were this, that, and the other thing as he was, but only Yankee wove the web of obligations and fear, the "natural" aristocracy of the person who came up through the ranks in a certain way, and only he presented his particular solutions to problems that frequently did not exist, although he said they did, and beat the drum for years until they were well entrenched. It was a lovely performance, and I frequently chuckled over it. Even the times he was defeated, temporarily, would have been a permanent setback for any lesser man, but he just soldiered on, and whispered whatever he whispered to his corporate sponsors, and lo! there he was again, as if he had never been gone.

And nobody, as far as I know, ever questioned the source of his wealth. Remarkable. Only in America.

And then one day, after about twenty years, things changed. I had come back from one of my various trips around the country, to inspect various odd bits that proved never to actually be flying saucer wreckage, and I noticed that I was more tired than usual, and that my arms tended to go to sleep. Then a while after that I began to get dizzy spells, and shortly thereafter the dizzy spells became quite noticeable; I could hardly stand up without feeling the effects. Lying down became an exercise in increasingly careful motion. And my legs cramped at night. At first I could solve this by slipping out of bed and standing up for a minute or two, but then the cramps moved out of my calves into my thighs and feet, and did not yield to simple remedies. I began to seriously lose sleep.

I did not know what to do. I could not, I at first told myself, go to a doctor. I became very worried when it proved more and more difficult to get up from a chair—often it took me two or three tries. I was only glad that no one observed me; I did fire the cleaning woman. I did, in short, as much as I could, and when this proved insufficient, I thought to call in Henshaw.

Henshaw, whom I had not actually seen since that one day long ago, was a peculiar person. He was black, first of all, and that tended to isolate him; he was a doctor of veterinary medicine, and that tended to isolate him further, from the ordinary run of black man. Then, his interests were very broad, and he acted on them; he had traveled to many parts of the world, he had studied far beyond the basic requirements of the DVM degree, he loved grand opera, he painted with quite a bit of skill and had studied painting—in short, and I have just touched on the high spots, he would have been thoroughly hated by the average person even if he hadn't been black, which he was, and which he rubbed your nose in if he got the idea this made him in your eyes in any way inferior to you, honky.

Of course, nevertheless, Yankee had chosen him to dissect Chaplain Joro because he was much less likely to be believed than a white man if he attempted to . . . spill the beans. That was many years ago, when Henshaw had first turned up, with the barest beginnings of a private practice among the poodles and kitties of Georgetown. He was Yankee's family animal doctor, and of course had had his measure taken early by Yankee, as all who came in repeated contact with him did. I was taking a chance in contacting him with my problem, but I really had no choice. He was the only man besides Yankee who knew about me, and he was the only man who was a medical practitioner.

I called a taxi, making my selection at random, and had myself driven out to his house in the middle of the night. I left a note in his mailbox while the taxi waited and had myself driven to the Willard Hotel, from which I took another taxi home. It was the best I could do. I did not think Yankee detected me. Then it was wait for Henshaw to come to me.

He did. DVMs are not ordinarily asked to make house calls, so he had to presume that after all these years I had another corpse to dissect. The arrangement was that he would be on call in case we ever found another one. The fact that we never did was beside the point.

We sat in my living room, I behind a desk, Henshaw

draped over an upholstered chair, a black bag at his feet. I had not seen him since that day at National, long ago now. He had not much changed. He was a large man, who gave a sense of power and vitality, and who, besides his wife and six children, took an occasional flier on other women, very discreet. Every time he did it, he put himself further into my power; I kept a tap on his phones, of course. And Yankee must have done something analogous to that, from before the very beginning—kept the man on a string, until he needed him, and then one day called him and suggested he get in his station wagon and go out to Washington National Airport.

And the man had gone, because he had no choice. But that was not why he had thereafter stayed a contingency employee of the NRPA all these years; no, not once he had seen me. Wild horses, I think, could not have kept him away. But of course I kept the phone taps anyway.

I said: "Doctor, something serious is wrong with me."

He raised an eyebrow. "And that's why you chose such a roundabout method of getting in touch with me? And asked me not to talk about it, on the phone or otherwise?"

"Yes."

He sucked his front teeth. "Interesting."

"Doctor, I want you to examine me and determine what's wrong, if you can."

A peculiar look come over his charmingly ugly features. "You don't want the services of a physician?

Ah." Henshaw sat back and looked at me. He folded his hands on the knee presented by his crossed legs. "You know," he said, "it's been a long time coming. Your calling on me in this way. I didn't know if you ever would. I wasn't even sure I was right about you. But if I hadn't gambled, would I have this opportunity now?" He smiled without it getting to his eyes, which remained speculative and searching. "The opportunity to get his hands on a living one of you? How many men could say they had done that? No, I've waited"—and now he did smile, genuinely—"patiently. And now I'll have my reward." He reached down for his black bag. "All right, take off your clothes." And we began. "You know," he remarked, "it'll be quite a novelty, having a patient who can talk."

Finally he was done, and I put my clothes back on. He toyed with the vials of blood he had drawn. "Fascinating," he said in a distracted voice. "Altogether fascinating." He put the vials away, carefully, in his bag. He looked up. "We'll have to wait a few days until the lab results come back, before I can be sure. Even then, how sure can I be?" He closed his bag and sat down in the chair again. "Systemically, you're sort of human, but not very much. I don't think we have to worry about what the lab will make of your blood. They'll think it's some kind of exotic animal—which, of course, is what it is, from the human point of view. And I can't tell now what abnormalities are present, not that it'll help a great deal when the results are in, because neither you nor I will ever know what the normal structure is—unless, of course, in the fullness of time I get a healthy one of you to examine, but I don't think that'll ever happen.''

"I really don't care about any of that."

"I didn't think you did. I'm stalling for time." He pulled at his lower lip. "All right. You've got some sort of severe circulatory problem. I can't tell how severe, because I don't know what your normal blood pressure is . . . and neither do you. Shame you weren't a doctor. On the other hand, you wouldn't be here, would you? The point is it's obviously severe, or you wouldn't have those symptoms. And those symptoms are incapacitating you. Now—what's causing the symptoms? That's much more interesting. And even less ponderable, for the moment at least.''

He got up from the chair and walked around my apartment, while I watched him with every fiber of my being. He cupped his hands together behind his back and went from wall to wall, without ever really seeing them. "You're a very sick boy," he said to the empty air. "Very sick. And I don't know how much I'm going to be able to help you." He turned back to me. "Not that anyone else could help you as much as I can. But that may turn out to be cold comfort.''

"I may die."

"Yes," he said, "you may die. But you knew that, or you would not have called even me.''

—Never revealed.

STATEMENT II, DITLO RAVASHAN

The next several days were not pleasant for me, waiting. And the dizzy spells and cramps were worse than they had ever been. When Henshaw arrived at my office, I was more than ready for him.

He sat down, taking a sheaf of paper out of a file folder—the lab report. He flipped it open and read it silently—again, I presumed—and then looked me in the face.

"You know what a T-cell is?" he asked, and before I could say no, he shook his head. "No, you don't." He put the laboratory report aside. "All right. About five years ago, a doctor happened to mention a peculiar thing to another doctor. He had begun getting a number—small, but a number—of a mysterious viral infection from Haitians, hemophiliacs, homosexuals, and h'infants. He mentioned it because he had thought of this cute way to describe the correlation. What was not so cute was that the disease resisted all attempts to handle it; his patients, every one of them, were either already dead or were dying. And actually he was a little bit scared.

"So you can imagine how he felt when the other doctor said he was seeing the same thing.

"They were at a medical convention, so they checked as best they could. And a significant number of other doctors said they were seeing it too.

"The other thing was, it wasn't the disease itself that killed people. There didn't seem to be a clear-cut disease, as a matter of fact, although their blood work-ups all showed the same pattern. But the patients died of half a dozen different diseases; cancers and lung diseases, mostly—not particularly frequent cancers. What the viral infection could do, it shut down the immune reaction. After that, it was just a matter of time. The first disease that came along after that, the person died."

"How many died?" I asked.

He shook his head wearily. "All of them. After a time, all of them die. There are no survivors."

"None at all?"

"None. At all. Nobody knows much about it yet. But nobody survives it. And we can't be sure, but I think it attacks h'aliens, too. I think you've got it."

I looked at him incredulously. "You think *I've* got it? Why? Surely you must—"

"Be mistaken? Maybe."

There was something about the way he said it, the way he looked at me. "But you think I've got it."

"I'm afraid so."

"How did I get it?"

"Well, I gather your sexual habits—" He shrugged. "Sex seems to have something to do with it."

"Jesus Christ, if that's all it takes, this town ought to be a hecatomb!"

"No argument. Perhaps in time it will be." He shook his head. "I know you won't take much of an interest, but this does look very bad for the future of the human race." He laughed without humor. "And I can't tell anybody about it. Well, it'll emerge among the more sensitive part of the human community soon enough, I'm sure. It'll be among the heterosexuals; white male Anglo-Saxon Protestant heterosexuals. That'll take care of it . . . raise an outcry like you couldn't believe."

"How long have I got?"

He shook his head. "I don't know. A month, maybe. Maybe a week. Whatever your particular disease is, it seems well advanced."

"A week."

"It's hard to tell."

"A week," I repeated. I looked around the office. "Well." The thing was, how did we do a funeral in which the corpse was totally destroyed? Because if it wasn't, some medical examiner whom we did not control would grow very interested.

"Henshaw, you've got to help me."

"Yes, I do," he agreed. He shook his head. "Funny how it leads you to this day. Life. I decided I was different, and I *was* different, but it didn't help after all."

"What are you taking about?"

"I didn't take any precautions while examining you. Why should I? But the fact is, just by some minor action I don't even remember, I may have contracted it. On the other hand, maybe not. But we can't be sure. I called the lab and made careful inquiries, though, and none of their technicians got any of your blood in a cut. So *that's* probably all right."

"Wait a minute—"

"Oh, it's not as bad as all that," Henshaw said. "For example, you apparently had a long interval between exposure and reaching a critical stage. And someone exposed to you might have even longer—after all, you *are* an alien, and any number of things might have happened. No, I might not have been exposed at all. But on the other hand—" He shrugged, not too casually. "On the other hand, we're not even sure what to look for, exactly, in the blood of someone who hasn't reached criticality. So I can't be sure. So I can't stick it in my wife or anybody else, anymore, forever." He laughed, not amusedly. "Ain't that a bitch? Of course, your case is considerably worse than that, so I don't expect you to sympathize."

And I don't suppose I did. His case was even funny, in a way . . . spending the rest of his life wondering when the disease would break out in him, nagged by the thought that he might not have it at all. But not daring to take the chance. Yes, it *was* funny. But I thought it best not to laugh. The wave of dizziness would have been overwhelming.

"Listen," he said, "we don't want to tell [and he gave Yankee's real name]."

No, we didn't. I had been very right to take precautions. But I said: "Well, that's interesting. Why not?"

"I've thought about it," he said. "All I can see coming from it is a million questions, including among others what in the hell I was doing visiting you in your apartment. I'm not supposed to know you, beyond one contact a long time ago. And of course that was true, until recently."

"I see."

"I don't have to tell you what he's like."

No, he didn't. He was right. The questions would never stop. The trust, once thought to be broken, would not be restored. It was even possible an accident would befall Dr. Henshaw. I had no reason to believe that— but in the case of Yankee, the fact that I also had no reason not to believe it was something to be considered. "All right. Makes sense. And it certainly makes no difference to me, at this point."

So we left it at that. I sank back in my chair, and the world whirled and spun.

And the time came. I could not walk anymore, and my body would convulse in cramps that were indescribably painful. It was more than a week after the last time Henshaw and I spoke. It was less than a month.

Henshaw came for me. I looked around the apartment one last time. Then I emptied my pockets, because when I left this apartment for the last time, I would disappear without a trace. Disappear permanently, but in any case, without a trace.

I hoped Yankee would reason that my people might have come for me. I chuckled a little bit.

The NRPA would go on; in time, it might even develop a new parent organization. I laid my wallet down on top of the little pile on my desk, patted my pockets, and extracted one last item—a Democratic National Committee matchbook. I looked at it, smiled briefly, and laid it down. It gave the address—the Watergate complex—and a phone number.

Henshaw looked at it. "What the hell are you doing with one of those?" he asked, a little incredulously. "I didn't think you gave a damn about our politics."

I laughed. "I didn't get a chance to try it. There's a hot rumor around that a call girl ring is operating out of one of the spare offices there."

"You're shitting me."

I shrugged. "That's the word. But what's the difference? Neither one of us is ever going to give it a try." I turned to leave the apartment, and stumbled into his arms.

We drove to a Virginia farm, long abandoned, the track running through shrubbery and fallen fences, until we stopped at what remained of the yard. Henshaw shut off the engine and looked at me. Then he said "No point stretching it out" and opened his little black bag. He took out a hypodermic and a bottle, and filled the hypodermic. "Cyanide," he said. "It'll kill you very quickly."

"All right," I said.

"Anything you want to say?"

Was there anything I wanted to say? To have come all this way, and to end like this. I remembered the chaplain, and how I had questioned him as he was dying. "What is the meaning of life?" I had asked him, and he had finally answered, "Hurt." Or perhaps not. Really, it occurred to me, it was a question to ask a child, not a dying man.

"No," I said. It hadn't been a bad life, everything considered. I was beginning to recall one of its more pleasantly outrageous moments, with a woman beneath my face and another kissing her while I fingered—but that was when I felt the needle go into my arm, and very soon thereafter I was dead.

Henshaw pushed me out of the car, and drove it a little ways away. Then he got out, opened the trunk, and took out the two five-gallon cans of gasoline. He doused me with one of them, and set it alight. Then he retreated to the car until the flames died down, and poured the second can over what remained of me, and lit that, going back to the car again. Finally he came back and stirred the remains, until you could not have said what it was that had burned there. There were some bone fragments, but beyond seeing to it they were scattered, Henshaw did nothing further. He did not need to. And so I departed this life, far from home. But whether I was home or not, I had had a good life. A somewhat shorter one than I had anticipated, but I had had the money, I had had the girls, and nobody told me what to do. Is there, really, anything else? Are you sure?

—Never revealed. A.B.

CONVERSATIONS BETWEEN FUNCTIONARIES

#1: I don't get it. I went into the apartment, and there's nothing unusual there but a pile of clothes, with the stuff piled on top.

#2: You've got no clue as to where the occupant's gone?

#1: None whatsoever. Everything's got a light film of dust on it, so he's been gone at least a week.

#2: All right. Inventory the stuff, and come back in. Then I'll pass the word up.

#2: Well, the shit hit the fan when I made my report. He wants you to get together a crew of trustworthy guys, break into the Watergate, and scour Democratic National Committee Headquarters ASAP.

#1: You're kidding.

#2: No, I'm not.

#1: Christ, there's never anything in a national committee headquarters! It's a clerical office, for Christ's sake!

#2: Buddy, you know that and I know that, but apparently he doesn't. So I suggest you do exactly as instructed. Put together a crew—get a bunch of those Cuban exiles or somebody else that'll tend to be loyal. And get in there!

#1: Jesus Christ. Jesus Christ.

MORE CARS

So for a while, I was Christie. Once a month, or sometimes twice, I drove into Newark, and parked the car in another garage, and a man handed me a sealed envelope which I took back to Roland, riding the bus.

The trips fascinated me at first. There was so much to see—the farms, and the gradually larger and larger villages, and finally the city, which was actually a whole group of cities, of course; the only way you could tell you were in Newark, finally, was by a sign on one side of a street. This was before they finished the New Jersey Turnpike—in fact, it was before they finished a whole bunch of things. The Adams Burlesque Theatre was still going in downtown Newark; ah, it was all right. They stripped down to nothing sometimes. And the comics were great; really great. I even saw Joe Yule, who was Mickey Rooney's father.

But truth to tell, it began to wear thin after a while.

I wasn't getting anywhere. I got to Newark once or twice a month, but it was as if I were on an elasticized string; I always went back. And the thought of spending the rest of my life on the edge of the barrens was more than I could comfortably live with.

My English got good; I was reading a lot. My favorite was the car magazines, of course. I even wrote some letters, and they printed them; it was mostly pointing out errors in the journalism, at first.

I wasn't getting anywhere with Margery, either. I began necking with her, timidly at first and later with considerable warmth, and she enjoyed it as much as I did, but that was all. Roland Lapointe just shook his head. "Look, you do know what it's for, don't you?" was as far as he went in commenting. I nodded, my face flaming, and he threw a bolt into a bucket on the other side of the garage and walked out.

One thing I learned from the burlesque was that Earthwomen had essentially the same equipment I was more or less familiar with. And I finally got my hands on one of Roland's nudist magazines, and found out my equipment was not essentially different from what Margery was accustomed to. But somehow . . . I don't know. It just . . . well, it might have gone on forever, I suppose, but one time I came back from Newark at dawn and found the light on in the back garage.

It was dawn. Roland never got up at dawn; he worked mostly at night. So the chances of the light having gone on recently were very low. But it was just as unusual for Roland to work *through* the night. In fact, he had never done it.

I looked at the window for a long time. Then I cautiously opened the door, and first thing that struck me was the smell. It reminded me, in a way, of the spots in Nick Olchuck's barn where the cats and the rats had been. But this was fresher. I went around the stuff piled in the front of the garage to look harmless through the window, and there was Roland, dead.

He *was* tough. The car had slipped off a jack and put a brake drum in the center of his chest. If the wheel had been on the drum, he might have lived. Even then, from the blood and the torn-up fingers it was clear he had been hours dying, his chest all concaved, but trying to push the car off to the end, dying, finally, in the small hours of the night, alone and thinking God knows what. I looked at him for a long time, and a lot went through my mind.

But really my choices were very few. I couldn't keep the operation going, and I couldn't expect to keep the garage . . . I couldn't expect anything. And I realized it was my big chance.

I backed out of the garage and closed the door. Then I went over to Roland's car, and the keys were in it, as they always were. I drove over to Margery's, and threw pebbles at her window. When she finally opened the window, tousle-headed and with her breasts falling out of her nightgown, I said: "Let's go."

She blinked. "What?"

"You coming with me?"

She blinked again. Her glance grew sharp. She took in Roland's car, and the sealed envelope sticking out of my pocket, and she bit her lower lip, but she nodded. Twenty minutes later we were on our way, headed for the Pennsylvania Turnpike, and I was explaining. It didn't take much. "All right," she said, "I've got it."

"One more thing."

"What's that?"

I carefully did not look at her. "Will you marry me?"

She said nothing for quite a while. Then she began to laugh. "Sure. Why not? Somebody's got to make an honest man out of you."

"I didn't mean to make a joke," I said.

She bit her lip. "No, I don't suppose you did." She looked at me in the morning sunlight while the car zipped along. "Neither did I, really." Her eyes were grave. "Yes, I'll marry you. For richer or poorer. For better or for worse." Her mouth quirked up. "I'll even throw in till death do us part; how about that, Jack, my Mullica Jack?"

I studied her. "I hope to make you happy."

She shook her head, staring off at nothing. "I think you've already done as much about that as you could," she said. "It's quite a bit, you know. Don't try to do any more than you can."

I didn't say anything. We would see.

We were married in a little chapel in Sandusky, Ohio. "You may kiss the bride," the beaming JP and the beaming witness said, and I did. Then we moved to the Lake Vista Motel, and there the pattern of our life together was established forever. I looked at her bleakly in the morning light, and she looked back at me and shook her head slightly.

"It doesn't matter that much, Jack," she said.

"Maybe it'll be better as I get used to you."

"Maybe. The big point is, I'm warm, I'm comfortable, and I know you love me."

I smiled a little. We were on the bed, stark naked, and she looked so desirable, so much the woman— Well, it wasn't as if I hadn't satisfied her, because I had. And it wasn't as if I hadn't ejaculated, because I had. But it was also true that I had no idea how she felt to be inside of, which made me practically unique among the men she had known.

"Jack—"

I let my grin widen. "What the hell? It wasn't so bad."

She laughed in turn. "No. No, it wasn't." She wriggled on the bed. "In fact, if you felt like some more, I could use—" Well, that's as much of that as you need to know. Gradually, over time, we accommodated. The time also came when she stayed out a little late, and after that, for all the years we were together, there were times when she stayed out. But she always came back. It was all right. Really.

We settled down in Detroit. I got a job in a garage—just cleaning up, at first, but eventually I got to be the lead mechanic—and she got a series of jobs as a supermarket cashier and so forth. Nobody ever came for us. What happened to Nick Olchuck we never knew, but the assumption is he vanished into a bottle. Roland's car we left on the street, miles away from the first apartment we got, and nobody ever connected us to it. I went by it a couple of times, and first the tires were gone, and then the hood and trunk were open, and then the engine was gone, and in about a week—this was before Detroit got real bad, which was why it took so long—all that was left was the frame and the body shell. So that was all right. And we lived.

We lived not badly. Both of us were making good money. I was making a bit on the side; *Automotive News* ran some of my fillers, and some of the other magazines. And then one day, in the classified section of the *News*, was an ad for an entry-level position in the public relations department of the number three carmaker. I was I guess a little bit older than most of the other applicants, but I had a track record established, and the man who would be my boss liked the way I wrote, and so I became an automotive PR man.

It was not glamorous. All the glamor is on the outside. It was cranking out press releases about the new rear axle ratio, and the rejetted carburetor, and like that, and you had to go to the engineers for the raw data. Engineers do not particularly like PR men. The senior

PR men got to stand around test tracks in suits and ties without a spot on them; we grunts had to find someplace that would wash a car at six in the morning in some godforsaken hole on the day of a press conference. More than once, I've mopped off a boss's car with the T-shirt torn from my own body, hosing down the piece with a hotel loading dock hose. And turned up at eight A.M. impeccably dressed, except I wasn't wearing an undershirt, handing out press kits to contemptuous automotive journalists, and secretly wondering if the engineers had actually had time to get the units into halfway decent shape. I remember the time we sent off the automotive editor of a major magazine to drive back to Long Island and test the hot new brakes on a completely new model; after he was gone, it turned out the engineers hadn't gotten delivery on the hot new brakes, so they substituted a set from the old model. We heard about that— we heard about that a great deal, and oddly enough it wasn't the engineers' fault, somehow; it was the PR department's.

But everything that doesn't outright kill you will eventually go away. One day they offered me the top job in the Chicago shop of the PR department, and I took it, because it was a good deal of money, and Margery and I moved to near the Borrow Street El stop in Shoreview. We lived in a nice condo overlooking the lake, and not even Selmon's eventually turning up really spoiled it, though I will admit I began hitting the bottle a little harder. But even that wasn't bad enough to really matter. I had made it—I was an American named Jack

Mullica, I had a good job, a wife, Margery, and I was home free.

Even after Selmon died—God, I felt sorry for the poor dumb son of a bitch!—I was home free.

—Reconstructed. A.B.

THE END

It was August, and Jack Mullica was home, idly watching TV. He was on sick leave. At a press conference in Lake Geneva, Wisconsin, at nine at night or thereabouts, he had been out on an airfield, checking the lineup of cars for the next morning's exhibition. Somehow one of the cars had been left idling, and somehow it had dropped into gear. (The PR department of course denies that ever happens, so the incident was tightly suppressed.) At any rate, the car had brushed Jack while he was paying attention to something else, and he had a badly bruised shoulder and arm. He was wearing a home-style sling on the arm and was doped up on Margery's Darvon now; that was all right—there wasn't anything to that, although he didn't much care for the close approach to getting something broken and being taken to a doctor. But he was convinced it had been a simple accident, and was not liable to be repeated.

Margery was out somewhere. Jack was watching President Richard Nixon getting into a helicopter in the middle of the day, and thrusting his arms out to each side with his fingers spread into a V. His family was around him. Jack frowned. Where was Nixon off to now, when he ought to be staying in Washington and putting down this Watergate scandal? Jack was about to bring more of his attention to the whole business—he thought the TV had made a reference to President Gerald Ford; what they must have meant was Vice President—when the doorbell rang.

Margery's forgotten her keys or something, Mullica thought as he made his way to the front door. Came into the building on someone else's ring, and now she's standing outside, waiting for me to let her in. He opened the door, and there was Hanig Eikmo. He gaped at him, and Eikmo, who was bent a little oddly, and wearing a suit from K Mart or someplace like that, and needed a shave, said in a hasty voice: "Can I come in?"

"Well—well, sure," Mullica said, and stepped back. He could not close his mouth. How in the hell had Eikmo—it was Eikmo, wasn't it?—he peered at the man as he came in and pushed at the door behind him, Mullica giving ground—yes, of course it was Eikmo, and somewhere in his system Mullica realized the Darvon was affecting him more than he had thought.

"Can I sit down?" Eikmo was saying, and once again Mullica said "Why, sure," and Eikmo sat on a straight chair, ignoring the overstuffed sofa.

"How are you, Dwuord?" Eikmo said. "Things going well for you?'' And Mullica belatedly realized Eikmo was speaking in their old language.

He pushed the language forward, speaking it for only the second time in years. "I—how did you find me?" Mullica was gathering himself, getting his presence back.

"Well, Selmon was writing to me once a month— payments, sending back the money he owed me. In the course of that, he told me you were here. Crazy. Policy violations like the plague, around here. Why the hell didn't he move away? But then the letters stopped coming." Eikmo looked around. "You alone? Nobody lives or visits here except for your lady?"

Mullica nodded. Eikmo looked around him again, and relaxed to a great extent. "Nice. I was settled in pretty well, too, but not like this. Wife died a little while ago. Not too much of a surprise; she was a lot older than me." Eikmo's voice grew softer for a moment. "I liked her a lot. Came from someplace near where we originally crashed. Funny. Coincidence. But she left the barrens years before we got there. Well, anyway—I came out here looking for Selmon. Had to know what had happened to him. And I found out what happened. Finding you wasn't that hard. I've been following you for about a week. When I saw your lady go out a while ago, I came up."

"Look, Eikmo, it's nice to see you, but policy—"

Eikmo laughed. "Policy! You haven't sold them the shoes and a dozen other things? The razor?"

"Christ, I use an electric shaver. What are you talking about?"

Eikmo laughed. "Sure. You don't know a thing about it."

"Oh, come on, Eikmo—"

Eikmo stood up. "It doesn't really matter what you say, does it? I'll take care of you. Living high on the hog. Killing Selmon." He slipped a long, sharp knife out of his sleeve. "What's the matter with you?" he shouted suddenly. "Killing a poor harmless man like Selmon!"

"I didn't kill Selmon!" Mullica cried out in protest, but at the same time he turned his body, and so the knife, which should have gone into his belly, sliced instead through his right forearm muscle, glanced off his equivalent to a radius and ulna, continued upward to the elbow, and jammed there, caught in the joint.

"Jesus!" Mullica cried, and fell back, spouting blood, confused, conscious that he could not bend either arm now, seeing the blood painting the corridor walls, stepping back farther.

"Leave me alone!" he blurted, falling into a couch, trying to find the pressure points in his forearm with the fingers of his left arm, which were dreadfully weak.

"You killed Selmon," Eikmo repeated, grappling for the knife.

"No! It was an accident. Why would I kill him?" It was a nightmare. Mullica turned his head this way and that, trying to find something that would help him, insanely watching Nixon's helicopter fly away. He didn't know if he should stop the flow of blood before he stopped Hanig Eikmo somehow; probably. Things came and went in his head with unnatural speed. He tried to hold on to one thought, any thought, and he couldn't, he couldn't.

Eikmo had his hands around Mullica's throat; Mullica was vaguely conscious that Eikmo had his knee in Mullica's lap.

"No! This is ridiculous, Eikmo! Help me stop the blood—"

"No. I'm not gonna help you stop the blood."

Mullica, in a panic, threw Eikmo off. He backed away from Eikmo, across the room. Eikmo came after him—an older Eikmo than Mullica remembered, but Eikmo, Jesus, Eikmo, he was supposed to be in Oakland, and instead—"Why, Eikmo?"

Eikmo had another choke hold. "What the hell did you kill him for?"

"I didn't—"

Now they were crashing through the doors to the balcony. And now he felt the railing pressing into his back. And now he was going over, and Eikmo was leaning on the railing, looking down at him, and getting smaller.

Margery came home. The front door was pushed shut, but the lock hadn't quite found the striker plate. The apartment wall was covered in blood. She dropped the grocery bag and sprang forward. She saw a man leaning over the balcony rail. She cried out, or rather, she sucked in air, and the sound of it was a voracious rattle in her throat. She was on the balcony in a split second, and as a startled Eikmo began to turn, she placed both hands flat on his chest and pushed. No one on Earth could have resisted that push. Eikmo went toppling into space, only moments after Mullica, and crashed down through twelve floors of emptiness before impacting on the concrete sidewalk, almost exactly on the spot where Mullica lay. And finally Margery cried out; it floated down, hard on the sodden thump of Eikmo's body. "Jack! Oh, Jack Mullica!"

Mullica saw the sidewalk coming up at him at an amazing rate of speed. Then there was a moment's blackness, and then he was looking up, and Eikmo was hurtling down at him. Jack rolled out of the way. His sling and the knife were gone. He looked up, and Margery was standing there, many floors above the street, shouting something, and then he was up there, holding her in his arms, and she was looking at him with all the love in the world, and he was taking her in his arms, and she was crying with joy, saying "Oh, Jack Mullica! Oh, Jack Mullica," so he took her into the bedroom and took her in his arms, and she was tearing off her clothes and his, and he was huge, he was godlike, and they made love, and they made love, and they made love, while she kept murmuring "Oh, Jack Mullica!" over and over again, wild and wanton, in his arms, beautiful in love.

—Never revealed. A.B.

Henshaw shook his head imperceptibly. He had told the widow he was with a government agency, which was true enough. Still, one had to be careful.

It was some days after the double death. The blood in the apartment had been partly cleaned up. There was new glass in the balcony doors, though the doors themselves were splintered in places and only temporarily repaired. The widow did not look good, which Henshaw found a fleeting moment to regret, because she was basically a fine-looking woman. But he was still not certifiably clear of the disease. They still didn't know much about it. They were beginning to suspect a long incubation period. It really didn't matter, to him; he was going to play with nothing but his hand for the rest of his life, and that was that. And, besides—well, besides.

The widow sat at one end of the couch, very small, somehow, very much in need of something she would not get. She looked at nothing. An open decanter of scotch, mostly used up, sat on the end table. A glass, mostly drunk, was in Margery Mullica's hand. She cried and she looked at nothing.

A television set was on, ignored, just something to fill the room a little. Henshaw actually looked for a moment, and saw that Gerald Ford had pardoned Richard Nixon. He shook his head incredulously.

"Mrs. Mullica," Henshaw said gently.

She looked at him with faint interest.

"Mrs. Mullica, I'll be going in a minute." And leaving you completely alone. "It's self-defense. That's clear. You'll be all right. But can you tell me *why* you pushed the stranger over the rail? Can you tell me that?" There were so many other things she could have done. True, most of them wound up with the stranger killing her, too. But still—

She smiled wanly, and looked at the drink in her hand. Then she looked at Henshaw. "I loved him," she said. "I didn't care. He fixed my leg. And he was the most decent man I ever knew. Or ever will know. Even if he was a Russian deserter. I didn't care where he came from." She was sort of smiling, and sipping at her glass, but she had not actually, at any time, stopped crying. "I didn't care where he came from," she said again. "I cared what he was. I will never find a man like him again," she said softly. "Never, never, never." And she continued weeping.

—From Henshaw's unwritten novel.

Well, there you have it. I began to research this book after the media story came out about two men falling off a condominium balcony. The TV and the papers covered it, of course, but something about the story didn't quite ring right. I figured it was worth a look. And the first thing I found, of course, was the blood all over the apartment wall—which nobody else had mentioned, and which I saw only because the superintendent happens to be my cousin. With that much to go on, I was off.

I'm sorry the book isn't more definitive. Actually, much of what precedes this closing note had to be made up. Well, all right, call it a docudrama, instead of the documentary that'll never be written because there's just plain so much that *has* to be conjecture. I mean, all five of them are dead, and were dead before I started on the book. Marjorie finally told me what she knew, for the most part, but when you look at it, she didn't really know very much, did she?

In fact, I could have made up the *whole* thing, couldn't I?

—A.B.